NAILED

By

JENNIFER LAURENS

Grove Creek Publishing

This is a work of fiction. Names, characters, places and incidents are either a product of the author's imagination or are used fictitiously, and any resemblance to actual persons, living or dead, business establishments, events or locales is entirely coincidental.

A Grove Creek Publishing Book/published by arrangement with the author.
NAILED, second edition
Grove Creek Publishing edition/Oct 2008

Cover artwork: Sapphire Designs
http://designs.sapphiredreams.org/
Book design: Julia Lloyd, Nature Walk Design
ISBN 978-1-933963-86-0
Printed in the United States of America

for my girls

NAILED

chapter one

FIRST JOB

Mandy hadn't taken the job framing houses so she could stare at tan, bare-chested hotties in low-riding jeans with tool belts slung around their waists. She'd grown up on construction sites—her father's workers and crew were like her uncles.

She was eighteen now, and the young guys glistening under the noon sun looked anything but related to her.

Her mouth went dry.

There were four golden gods in all. One was her brother Marc. She wasn't looking at him, of course. She was watching his nail-toting, hammer-wielding companions. All three, including her brother—even though she cringed at the admittance—were built better than any sculpture she'd seen. She couldn't take her eyes off their muscle flexing under golden-brown skin.

The sun was hot, with rays that needled her. Her arms, naked in the tank top she was wearing, felt the heat, though she was sure half of it was due to the sizzling sight. The guys had on shorts, their legs the same rich bronze as their bodies. She'd worn jeans because of the potential hazards on the job, and was sorry now—the sun's fire magnified through the denim. She'd be a walking oven in no time.

I need to focus, Mandy blinked as if that would cause the exquisite scene before her to vanish. She cleared her throat.

The sound brought all heads whipping her direction.

"Hey." At least her voice didn't betray her rattling nerves.

Her brother scowled and started over to her. He jerked his sandy head her direction and the other guys immediately left their posts and crossed to her.

When Marc stopped, she recognized the musky odor of his sweat, like a signature.

"This is my sister, Mandy," he announced. The three other guys approached in what Mandy could have sworn was slow motion…in her head she heard a bass thumping, drums pounding, as if the moment was straight out of a music video.

The first guy had a red bandana wrapped around his head. The laugh lines feathering away from his smiling eyes told Mandy that he was probably the oldest of the group, somewhere in his late twenties. He most definitely was the tannest, his skin starting to leather.

He extended a hand. "A.J. Heard a lot about you. Congrats on graduating."

His hand was hot and sweaty, but Mandy expected that. "Thanks."

Next to A.J. stood a buzzed blond with pearl-blue eyes. He hadn't shaved, Mandy noted, and the stubble on his cheeks and neck made him look like he was a surfer who'd just taken a wave and brought home some sand. His light denim, thread-bare shorts were cut off at the knees, the hems frayed. He rubbed his hand on his rear pocket before sticking it her direction. "Larry."

Mandy gave him a nod when she shook his hand. "Hey."

The last one of the crew looked to be about her age, and from the intense focus of his deep brown eyes she knew he was about as happy as Marc to have her there. He wore a blue Boston team baseball cap over hair nearly the same rich chocolate color as his eyes. He was forgoing the friendly handshake by keeping his arms crossed over his chest.

Mandy withdrew her extended hand. Marc had squeezed enough lemons into her life that she never puckered up and backed away from anything. "You going to tell me your name or do I call you Boston?"

His eyes narrowed. "Boston will be fine."

"Nice to meet you, Boston."

"It's Charlie," Marc said.

Mandy wondered why Boston shifted, like he was embarrassed, at the mention of his name. "Charlie? As in Charles?"

"As in Charlie," Boston corrected.

"I'll stick with Boston," she grinned. "Now, where do you want me?"

The guys exchanged slow glances. Marc sighed, scratched his shaggy hair and looked her over from pony tail to work boots. "You can back out now and I won't tell Dad a thing."

Mandy stiffened. "Forget that."

"Man." Marc shook his head. "I can't believe you're trying to do this."

"I'm not trying, Marc, I'm doing. Now tell me where you want me. Or maybe you'd prefer it if I call Dad and get my instructions from him." She whipped out the cell phone she kept in her belt.

"This isn't *his* job," Marc snapped. "It's *my* job."

"Don't worry, I won't step on your boots." She tucked the phone back with a smile. "Just tell me where to go."

The guys chuckled and exchanged low murmurs Mandy was sure weren't complimentary. "Something you want to say?"

A.J held up his palms. "Not me, sister." He looked at Marc. "I'm getting back to work, boss." With a wink and whistle, he turned and headed to the northern most corner of the partially framed house.

"Uh, yeah…" Larry scrubbed his stubble as he backed away. "That goes for me."

Mandy's eyes widened when he turned and she saw his backside; the denim was so worn it barely held together over grey knit bun-huggers. When he reached back for a deep crack scratch, her face twisted.

She knew better than to verbalize disgust, and when she tore her gaze away from Larry's barely-covered bottom she found both Marc and Boston watching her. Marc wore a smirk, but Boston's expression was dark and unreadable.

Mandy stood erect, one hand poised on her hammer, the other on her drill. "Shall we?"

Marc sighed. "Come on, then." He took off, and she followed, noting Boston's gaze was still locked on her. She stopped.

"After you." Mandy made a sweeping gesture. This guy had a nail stuck in his cheek, it was obvious.

Finally, he uncrossed his arms, and Mandy couldn't help that her eyes were drawn by the gravitational pull of his ripped abs. Before she let her gaze linger, she cleared her throat and looked him in the eyes.

His not-amused expression told her he didn't appreciate being sized up. Lifting her chin, she decided to slip on her boxing gloves. She'd learned a lot growing with a brother who loved to remind her how inferior the female sex was. She could fight as long and hard as the next guy.

Marc's angry voice broke their tight stare down. "Over here, Mand. Now."

Mandy avoided stray blocks of wood, fallen nails, and other potentially hazardous debris as she made her way to her brother. She kept glancing over her shoulder, feeling the quiet heat of Boston at her heels.

"Ready, boss." Playfully, she whipped out her hammer and drill, but the joke only made Marc's face stony.

"You can start bringing over sheers," he told her. "We'll be going up tomorrow."

Seeing that he was finally going to let her do her part, she dropped the antics and nodded, slipping her tools back into the belt.

"Supplies are—"

"I know." Why he was explaining the basics, she couldn't fathom, unless it was to show his team he was good at bossing around. She and Marc had grown up playing in framed houses like monkeys on a jungle gym.

Marc snorted, looked at Boston and jerked his head, and the two of them walked off to another section of the house. Mandy let out a little huff.

She pulled leather work gloves out and slipped them on. No way was she going to ruin a fresh set of acrylic nails she'd just had put on two days ago.

Crossing through the site, she stopped and took in a deep breath. She loved the smell of raw wood, the sound of hammers banging—that magical rhythm that was both passionate and fierce, uncivilized like the melody of a tribal sacrifice deep in the jungle. Ever since she was a little girl that scent had intoxicated her, the act of constructing had enticed her, and she'd decided to set her course for her own construction company someday, just like her father.

"Smell the roses on your own time." Marc's cross voice snapped through her bliss. She cocked her head at him. She'd paused for what, about a second?

"Yes, sir," she said with a salute. A.J and Larry hadn't stopped to take note of their little squabble, but Boston had. She gave him a friendly nod before making her way off the cement foundation and onto the dirt. If these guys thought she was going to cave under a little rough treatment they had another thing coming.

The thigh-high stack of four-by-eight pieces of plywood lay just outside of the framed first floor. She reached over, put both hands on the sides of the top piece and pulled. It weighed a ton, and she grunted, levering the rough wood so it slid off the pile and stood upright.

Her quick glance back at the guys reminded her that she had an audience: all of them had stopped and were watching. She blew her bangs out of her eyes and gripped the cumbersome piece, lifted it about four inches and started over.

The muscles in her arms quivered and sweat streamed down the sides of her face, along her spine.

It wasn't as though she couldn't carry the twenty-five pound weight. It was the awkward position she had to carry it: right out in front of her. Most workers hauled sheers over their heads. She'd never be able to do that.

By the time she had the piece near the corner where they were working, she was gasping. Resting it against one of the framed walls, she stepped back and swiped her forearm across her forehead.

"Gee," Marc began, and Mandy knew by his tone he was going to be mean. "That only took you seven minutes. At this rate, we might have the first floor done in, what, about four weeks?"

Mandy glared at him but didn't say anything, just stomped back to the pile and grabbed another one. She tried to hold the sheer up higher in hopes she could cross the site faster, but the awkward position left her waddling like a duck so her knees didn't bump into the sheer. She only made it halfway before she had to stop and give her arms a much needed break.

Refusing to look at Marc or the other guys, she hoisted up the plank again and labored over to the wall then laid this piece against the other.

"Aw, come on." A.J. set down his nail gun, stepped away from the wall he was framing and sauntered over with a grin.

"You – don't – need – to help me," she gasped. "I can do – it myself."

"Sure you can, baby doll." He was over at the pile of plywood before she could say another word. With the effort of plucking cardboard, he had two pieces of the bulky wood off the pile and up over his head. His eyes crinkled into another grin. "You pull 'em off the stack and

I'll carry them over, how's that?"

Mandy blinked. One glance at her brother and she knew he'd chide her later. "That's nice of you, A.J., but I can do this. If it takes me all day, I will do this."

"It'll take you more than all day," he winked. "And I know you'll do it. But it's a two-man job, so, I'm your man." He started back into the house, every muscle in his body snapping to attention under the load.

Over in the corner, Marc shook his head and went back to work. Larry started whistling. The look of wary curiosity on Boston's face had Mandy lifting her chin and staying locked in another stare-down with him until he finally turned, driving his hammer fast and hard at a two-by-four.

A stream of frustration ran through her. So this was it? Her dream of working for her dad, of learning his trade was going to be earned with teeth and nails? Power games and politics?

A.J. tossed the sheers into the stack she'd started and headed back her direction. Quickly, she reached over, grabbed onto another piece of plywood and pulled it off the stack, then held it ready. His fingers brushed her gloves and he smiled into her eyes before taking the piece. "What, they didn't have enough room for you at Harvard?"

Mandy flushed. "They did. I just...I've always wanted to build houses."

"That so?" A.J.'s smile deepened. "Guess that's why you're here then."

"That's right." Mandy gave a nod, hoping the others, including Marc, would get over it. "It's been my dream since I was a little girl."

"Dream, huh? Well, baby doll." A.J. took the sheer and lifted it. Sweat glazed the contours of his chest and underarms. "You came to the right place." He turned and headed across the site. "Didn't she boys?"

"We're it, yeah," Larry piped with a string of nails propped between his teeth before pounding his hammer. He laughed, and the guys laughed with him.

Mandy went back to work.

In tandem, they moved half the pile, until A.J. stopped, yanked the red bandana off his head and swiped it over his face. A crop of caramel-colored hair stuck up on end and he scrubbed it with a groan of pleasure. Mandy pulled her water bottle from the back of her tool belt and took a long drink.

By noon, Marc, Larry and Boston had finished half of the main floor framework.

"I'd say it's about lunch time, wouldn't you, boss?" A.J. addressed Marc.

Marc glanced at his watch. "Yeah, it is."

Though Mandy acted like she could go on until midnight, her arms were ready to fall off and she had a dull ache in her lower back. One sweep of the toned, sweaty bodies surrounding her and she humbly realized she had a long way to go before her own body could take long days of abuse like this. But she was okay with that. *This isn't a race, but a marathon.* She didn't care if she was at the starting line and these guys were already half way around the track. She'd catch up. She might even pass them by.

Each of the guys took off their tool belts and started toward the white *Homes by Haynes* truck Marc had driven them to the site in. They gathered at the rear of the vehicle and laid their belts inside the bright metal box meant to safely store valuables under lock and key.

Mandy joined them. Standing behind a wall of bronzed males she was overcome with the musk of perspiration – hers, mixed with the fading, sweet perfume she'd dabbed on earlier and their natural scents heavy and dirty, but not entirely disgusting. Mandy understood a fair amount of stink came with the job. She cleared her throat, and waited for the wall of flesh to part so she could safely stow her own belt.

A.J. turned around and flashed a glimpse of white teeth. Before she knew it, he had her belt and was setting it inside of the storage box for her.

She caught Marc rolling his eyes. He pulled a red *Homes by Haynes* tee shirt over his head. She had to defend herself. "Thanks, A.J., but you don't have to treat me any differently than you would one of the guys. Really. I can take care of myself."

"Just helping out." A.J. snatched another red company tee from a pile in the truck bed. His chest rippled in fast, hard waves as he slipped it on.

Larry reached over, snagged a shirt and moved past her to open the door of the cab. "Let's roll, I could eat a horse."

Slamming the storage lid, Marc locked it, then rounded the truck and got into the driver's seat. After adjusting his baseball cap, Boston climbed up over the bed of the truck, and tugged on a shirt before stretching out using the pile of leftover tee shirts as a pillow.

A.J. tilted his head toward the cab. "You coming to lunch, baby doll?"

"Sure." She was part of the crew, why wouldn't she?

Mandy followed him to the cab. He held the door open and gestured for her to get in. With two big guys already scrunched inside, there was barely enough room for A.J. Marc's glare almost had her backing out of lunch altogether.

"Sometime today, Mand," Marc bit out.

She climbed up. A.J. shut the door and his muscled body nestled next to hers, nudging her against Larry. Because they were crammed like sardines in a can, A.J. stretched out his arm behind her back.

"See? Little thing like you can fit anywhere," A.J. smiled.

"Thanks for making room."

"You're one of us now." A.J. patted her shoulder. "Where we go, you go. Right, boss?"

"Uh, right." As soon as Marc started the car, Aerosmith blared from all four speakers. Mandy didn't miss the teasing smile Marc shot at A.J. as he pulled the truck out onto the street. A truck full of construction workers and she was the only girl? She had a feeling they wouldn't be dining at Wendy's.

• • • • •

Five notes off-key, A.J. sang with Steven Tyler as the truck rumbled along. He was the kind of guy who did what he wanted, and Mandy liked that.

"So you work construction because *American Idol* turned you away?" she teased.

He grinned, nodded. "You got it." And he kept singing.

Marc wore his usual scowl. She couldn't understand

why he seemed so miserable. Like her, he'd wanted to work for their dad's company. Like her, he'd joined a crew right after he'd graduated from high school two years ago. Now, he had his first crew and his first job as foreman. He was currently girlfriendless, maybe that was the problem. But then his girlfriends never stuck around very long because he was such a grouch. Go figure.

Larry was tuned out. His pearly-blue eyes fixed out the front window as if he was hypnotized by the long stretch of road they were driving on.

Once they had driven out of the residential area of Saratoga Springs, Mandy noticed that Marc was driving them to the newer retail section of town. Good, there'd be a lot to choose from to eat. Pizza was her favorite, but she could handle a double bacon cheeseburger right about now, too. *Mmm.* And a nice, frosty chocolate shake. Her stomach let out a cascade of growls right between Sweet Emotion and Rag Doll.

A.J. tapped her. "You hungry?"

"Yeah, I am, actually."

"I could eat a horse," Larry said.

Mandy cocked her head. "Just one? I would have thought you could eat two by now."

Larry's eyes shifted to hers.

"They have horses on the menu where you're taking us, Marc?" she asked.

Marc covered a grin by scrubbing his jaw. "Uh, yeah."

"*Big* horses," A.J.'s smile wasn't any less teasing, and Mandy saw her first red flag.

The new strip mall wasn't even full of retailers yet, but it had one of Mandy's essentials: a Barnes and Noble

Book Store. She often haunted the place late at night when her friends were working or dating. It'd been a while since she'd been there, busy as she had been with the end of senior year. A dry cleaners, a Payless Shoe Store and a couple of boutique dress shops dotted the mall. The rest of the retail spots were still empty. She couldn't imagine where the guys planned to eat.

Then she saw it over in the far corner. Of course the parking lot surrounding the place was packed. She let out a smirk as Marc searched for an empty spot to park.

Brown, orange and white, the owl with perfectly round, boob-shaped eyes looked at her, mocking. Mandy took a deep breath. Leave it to Marc. No way was she going to appear ruffled.

"I love this place," she squealed.

Marc snorted and put the truck in park.

"They have the best..." She had to think for a second. She'd heard her guy friends talk about the chicken. "Wings here."

"The wings aren't the reason I come here," Marc chided, getting out. At least his scowl was gone, that was something.

"It's why I come here," Mandy piped, sliding out behind A.J. His teeth gleamed at her. "Yup, love those chicken wings," she said.

"You've never eaten here in your life." After everybody had piled out, Marc pressed the remote and locked the truck.

"I come here with Cam all the time."

"Right. This is the kinda place a gay guy would love."

"Cam is not gay."

"I have a feeling you'll do just fine here," A.J.

grinned.

"Yup." Mandy took a deep breath.

She was smack in the middle of the four guys as they walked to the entrance. Marc probably hadn't bought the story about her eating there before—with Cam—but she didn't care. If they were going to play, she'd play right along.

Marc pulled the door open and in typical brotherly fashion, went inside first. The social faux pas didn't go unnoticed by A.J., who held the door wide open for her.

"Thank you, A.J."

The place rocked. Between the loud music, sports-blasting TV's hanging from the ceiling, and bouncing bosoms of the waitresses in their orange shorts and tight tees, Mandy rated the raucous room about a seven on the Richter scale.

A brunette *Hooter* greeted them with a smile. "Welcome to *Hooters*. Party of five?"

Marc nodded. He looked amazingly chipper now, Mandy mused. The lot of them walked through the restaurant, passing tables packed with loud lunch diners, most of them men. Though she saw a few females, she felt out of place, and when some of the male diners were brazen enough to glance at her chest, she cringed and crossed her arms.

The *Hooters*' hostess sat them at a center table. *Super*, Mandy thought, *nothing like being in the spotlight*. A.J. pulled out a chair for her and she sat. "Thanks, A.J. Wow. Nothing distracts you from being a gentleman, does it? That's nice."

Because Boston had taken the seat to her left, Larry sat on her right and A.J. sat across from her, next to Marc.

"I grew up with four sisters." A.J. grinned.

"That explains it." Mandy opened her menu. She scanned the options, but she didn't miss Marc elbowing A.J. and pointing to a *Hooters* hottie working a few tables over.

Mandy stole a look. Tiny, blonde and bouncy, the woman was the typical bombshell that always caught her brother's eye. To her left, Boston focused intensely on the menu. He'd taken off his hat, probably right after they'd walked in, and now his deep chocolate-colored hair was matted against his head in the shape of a cap, the ends curled out and up.

"So, what's good here?" she asked him.

His onyx eyes slid to hers. "I thought you said you've eaten here."

His voice traveled through her on a slow wave. He'd said his name earlier when they'd first met, but that hadn't been enough for her to catch the low melodic cadence.

"Uh, yeah, I have. You just looked so…well, like you're really making a big decision. I thought you might have some suggestions. Or favorites."

His expression remained neutral and his gaze went back to the menu. "I like the Chicken Caesar salad." Then he closed the menu and set it aside. Chicken Caesar salad was bland for her liking, and Mandy settled on something hot and satisfying.

Mandy found the scene telling. A.J., Marc and Larry sat sprawled in their chairs, watching the waitresses come and go. Boston, on the other hand, sat upright, his serious face forward, his gaze straight ahead and undistracted more like he was seated in a classroom than a restaurant.

Marc was in luck. Blond bombshell wiggled over. "Hi, have you all been to *Hooters* before?"

Everyone said they had.

"What can I get you all to drink to start out with?"

Mandy wasn't surprised the guys ordered waters and soda. Everyone except Boston who ordered only water.

"I'll have a chocolate shake," Mandy said. "And could you add a little bit of roasted peanuts to that, please?"

Boston twirked his head her direction, what looked like amusement played on his face. "What?" Mandy shrugged.

"And for lunch?" The blonde batted her lashes, starting with Marc, who asked her what her favorite menu item was—*Hooters* famous wings—before ordering it. A.J. wanted the fried chicken plate. Larry asked for a platter of chili fries and Boston ordered the Chicken Caesar salad – dressing on the side.

Mandy didn't know any guys who liked salad, and stared at him with fascination.

The *Hooters* bombshell cleared her throat. Mandy looked at her. "Oh, I'll have a bacon double cheeseburger, fries and coleslaw."

Boston's dark eyes swept her with a quick look of disbelief. "Hey," she said, noticing the look, "some of us like to eat real food."

The waitress snapped the order on a cable overhead that ran directly to the kitchen, gave it quick tug, and sent it sliding off before she wiggled on her way.

"You really going to eat that, a little thing like you?" A.J. asked.

Mandy noticed the scowl was back on Marc's face. "She's always eaten like a pig."

"Marc." Mandy made sure her tone whipped.

"It's true." The glimmer of teasing in her brother's eyes didn't bother her, at least he wasn't scowling. "Ever since we were kids, she's packed it away like a cow. We have to bring her in every night so she stops grazing."

"I like a woman who appreciates a meal." A.J.'s nod was approving. "Too many think they have to eat to impress the men they're with."

"She's still a kid." Marc's gaze was now fastened on another waitress. "It'll catch up with her soon enough. Check it out. Nice."

Mandy didn't like that Marc refused to see her as an adult. One sweep around at the guys' faces, and she hoped they didn't all think that way. "I'm not the one with love handles."

The guys chided Marc, bringing a blush to his tanned skin. "This is steel under here." He caressed his abdomen in jest. "Pure, hard steel one hundred percent."

Mandy grimaced. "Ew, too much information."

A.J. and Larry laughed. To her left, Boston had a smile on his face, but Mandy couldn't tell if he was laughing or just pretending. "You're going to have to get used to hearing it raw." Marc's expression was cocky. "You're one of the guys now."

"I can handle it." Mandy plucked her napkin, opened it and set it on her lap. "It's nothing I haven't heard before. I've lived with you, haven't I?"

"She's a sassy one, isn't she?" A.J. chuckled.

"More than sassy," Marc sneered. "Pain in the butt is what she is." Marc's head turned. "Wow, check it out.

Baaayybee. Now that's the way a woman should be built. Perfect. Mmm, yeah."

Larry licked his lips. "Sweet."

Mandy followed Marc, Larry, and A.J.'s gazes to a redhead, shaped like a guitar, serving lunch to a table of hungry men two tables away.

She laughed in spite of herself. Guys were guys and there was just no getting around it. She caught Boston's determined profile. He didn't even turn around for a look at the redhead, and she wondered why.

chapter two

They baptized her right there at the table, immersing her in wild stories, raunchy jokes and crass language, peppered with words Mandy had never even heard before. Marc wasn't going to make anything pleasant or easy for her, that she knew going in. He still hoped she'd go whining home to Daddy about a scraped knee or a broken nail.

Through the course of lunch she learned that Larry went through women like he went through nails. The guys had a cash kitty that had grown to fifteen dollars over the last week, each of them putting in a dollar every time Larry had a new girl. Like Marc, A.J. was currently without a woman. A.J. had been working construction for the past seven years, since he'd quit his accounting job for the sole purpose of making money doing something with his hands. All of the guys were new to Haynes Construction, but claimed her dad was a better contractor than most out there.

Mandy loved hearing that.

None of the guys said much about Boston during the brief tell-all. Except when Marc cracked that he might as well be celibate, like Boston, for all the women he'd been able to keep lately.

"Celibate?" Mandy looked at Boston. No wonder he looked serious all the time. He had both hands on his glass of water, his long, tanned fingers glued to the frosty glass.

"He's sworn off females indefinitely," Marc piped.

"Man, I could never do that," Larry said.

"It's because you do the burning," A.J said. "Wait until it's you that gets fried." His gaze shifted to Mandy. "Charlie just got dumped."

So that was the reason for the stand offishness. Mandy eyed Boston's tight jaw. He picked up his glass and threw back an ice cube. His firm, wide mouth moved jaggedly. He stared straight ahead.

"I'm sorry," she said. He turned wary eyes to her. "No, I mean it. Some girls can be such idiots. Catty, self-serving, manipulative, jealous...If I were a guy, I'd be careful."

"You got that one down," A.J. agreed.

"Who are you? The voice of experience?" Marc couldn't pass up the opportunity to rub her nose in.

Mandy rolled her eyes. "I'm a girl and I know girls."

"Charlie's taking it to the extreme," Marc said through a grin. "I've seen him cross a street to avoid the opposite sex. I'm surprised you didn't bolt when the waitress took our order, man."

Boston smirked and shook his head. His dark eyes sparkled, and Mandy felt a quivering rush deep inside. She'd have given her tools to see him smile right then.

"I gotta hand it to him," A.J. began. "He's disciplined. More than I'd be."

"That night at the bar?" Larry started, and both Marc and A.J. laughed along. "We had to drag him there."

"Then he spent the whole night in a corner," Marc added. "Never mind all the babes that kept asking him to hook up."

"Yeah," Larry's grin spread. "He sent 'em to me. Thanks, dude."

Marc elbowed Larry. "And you could have shared, man."

"No way, you kidding?"

"Drop it," Boston's tone was sharp. He picked up his empty water glass and plunked it down again.

Marc slugged a hand playfully into Larry's bicep. "Guess you're going to see what it's really like to be a guy, Mand." He leaned forward with relish. "Every rough, slick, nasty detail."

Mandy rolled her eyes. "As long as it doesn't come from you. That's just twisted." Out the corner of her eye, Mandy thought she saw Boston give a fast nod of agreement then but she couldn't be sure.

The waitress brought over the check and Marc, Larry and A.J. all shot teasing grins at Boston who shifted in his chair, determination drawing his face tight. Another quivering rush shook Mandy. Everybody dug into their pockets and tossed their money to Marc.

"You all come back now, okay?" the blonde waitress bubbled.

"Oh, we will." Marc laid the cash in the bill fold and handed it back to her. "Keep the change, sweetheart."

Her eyes grew big when she looked at the money. "Thanks. Thanks a lot." With a swivel, she was gone.

Mandy stood. "Looks like you just bought yourself a date."

"You think?" Marc asked absently, watching the waitress's hips sway away. "I'll buy it. I got no shame."

Mandy nodded. "Oh, yeah. That's what fluff girls do

when they want a guy...act all cute and brainless."

The five of them started through the packed restaurant toward the door. A.J. smiled down at her. "Not you, though, right baby doll?"

Leading the pack, Mandy shoved the glass doors open with both hands. "Not this girl."

They worked until eight o'clock because it was daylight savings time, the guys wanted the overtime and none of them, except Larry, had plans for the night. As Marc predicted, they finished framing the entire main floor and were ready to start on the second story.

Working late was fine with Mandy. Most of her friends had all taken off on graduation road trips or other celebrations. They'd teased her because the only thing she wanted to do to celebrate was start working.

As the sun began to dip in the navy sky, the air cooled and a soft breeze came up.

Mandy enjoyed the slight drop in temperature. When she and A.J. carried the last sheer over and nailed it in place, she took a moment to catch her breath and savor the smell of wood. Closing her eyes, she lifted her arms over her head and clasped her elbows, enjoying the air cooling her under arms.

A bird cawed, the call vanishing on the wind. A dog barked. She loved the sounds of a quiet construction site almost as much as she loved the harmony of hammers, nail guns and the occasional skill saw.

Then it occurred to her – there were no hammers or nail guns. She opened her eyes and looked into the amused faces of A.J., Larry and Marc, all standing a few feet away. Boston was over in the corner, packing up some supplies for the night, but he glanced over just as she lowered her hands to her sides.

"You all right there?" A.J. asked.

"Uh, yeah. Just cooling off."

The guys exchanged smirks before heading to the truck.

"You want to get a drink?" A.J. stood with Larry at the back of the truck. Both were unbuckling their tool belts.

"Yeah, I could do with one."

Mandy joined them. "So, where we going?"

Larry laid his belt inside the metal case. "Uh..."

"You like booze, baby doll?"

Mandy ignored Marc's snicker. "I can drink my share."

"You've never even tasted the stuff," Marc teased.

A.J. took the belt from her hands, turned and put it away. Mandy felt the warm heat of a body behind her and looked over her shoulder at Boston.

"Okay, so I was just playing around." She batted lashes.

A.J. touched the tip of her nose with his finger. Then he moved aside so Boston could store his tool belt. "Sweet things like you don't want to hang in bars and places like that."

They were surrounding her again, cool, smooth skin and spent male scents that made her stomach whirl and her pulse skip. "Can't stand the stuff anyway. No worries there, A.J."

"So you have tried it." Marc cocked his head. "I

knew it, you little liar."

Mandy sent him a giant grin and backed toward her car, digging in her jeans for keys. "None of your business, Marcus. See you guys tomorrow."

"Yeah, but we leave at seven." Marc opened the truck door. "No more driving out to the site on your own, you know that's against policy."

"And you know where I'm concerned, Dad bends policy." She jiggled her keys with a teasing laugh that made Marc roll his eyes.

"Yeah, I know." Marc got in the truck and slammed the door. Then he rolled down the window. "As your supervisor," his tone dripped with sarcasm, "I'm telling you those rules won't bend as long as you're on *my* job, got it?"

Mandy saluted him. "Yes boss. See ya tomorrow, A.J. Larry."

A.J. nodded at her before he climbed into the cab next to Marc. Larry didn't say or do anything but get in and shut the door. Boston pulled himself up into the bed of the truck.

"See ya, Boston."

His dark eyes locked on her as he sat, arms stretched out along the rim of the bed. He lifted the bill of his cap in a gesture of good-bye that sent a nice tickle through her blood.

She enjoyed one more look at the quiet site, took in her last breath of wood, and got in her car. She figured she'd burned off the *Hooters* double bacon cheeseburger, fries and chocolate shake and then some. She drove through Taco Bell, grabbed a half-pound burrito, some Fiesta potatoes, a Pepsi, and headed home.

Summers in Saratoga Springs meant eighty-five plus temperatures most days. Even nights were warm. The valley, surrounded by tall, majestic mountains, created an oven effect.

She drove with her windows down and music loud. Though she appreciated all types, Sugarcult bounced from her speakers now and she bounced along, balancing her burrito in one hand, the potatoes in the other in between sips and steering.

Through chews she sang along, and her warbling reminded her of A.J. He was a lame singer, but she liked the guy. It was cool that he was older. He had manners. The world needed more guys like him. Maybe some of his class would rub off on Marc, though she doubted it. Their own parents were classy and that hadn't done much. Marc still preferred crass to culture.

A horn beeped somewhere just as she stuffed the last hunk of burrito into her mouth and Mandy turned to see who it was. Cam in his red Five Buck Pizza shirt waved from his tiny Toyota zooming the opposite direction.

Mandy waved back.

Like her, Cam hadn't traipsed off on some graduation indulgence, but had stayed home to work and put money aside for school. Some kids were just smarter, Mandy decided through a sip. You had to plan and educate yourself, or you'd end up a loser working some dead-end job the rest of your life.

Not her. She'd had her plans laid out like a set of blueprints since she was old enough to read and had chosen house plans over fiction. Graduate, go to school, and get her contractor's license, work for Haynes

Construction, and either take over Dad's company or start one of her own.

When her cell phone played a jumpy tune, she grinned and plucked it up. "Hey, Cam. How late are you working tonight?"

"Just through rush, why? Something up?"

"Not yet. Wanna meet later?"

"Yeah."

"K. Our spot?"

"Yeah."

"See you when you get there." She clicked off the phone, excited now that she was going to spend the evening doing her second most favorite thing other than working—hanging with one of her favorite friends. The night wasn't going to be a waste.

It wasn't that she didn't like being at home with her parents, she just preferred hanging out and since most of her friends had taken off on her, she'd been pretty solitary with the exception of Cam.

Since it was Friday, her parents were out on their customary dinner and a movie date. She parked in the driveway. She never tired of admiring the craft and quality of their two-story, stone and brick house her dad had built some ten years earlier. He'd built the four-thousand square foot house on spec, and because the housing market had been slow at the time, it hadn't sold. It wasn't for any other reason than that, because the house was appointed with every luxury and perfect detail any homeowner would want. They'd moved in and lived there ever since. She came to understand that building and business were different sides of the work.

She unlocked the heavy wood door and

deactivated the alarm system. Her dog, Scamper, flurried over in a ball of white and fawn-colored fur and leapt into her arms, then proceeded to lick her neck.

"You love that salty sweat, dontcha girl?" Mandy carried her up the terracotta tile stairs to the second floor, nuzzling her. "Well, I'm covered in it today."

She'd just reached the landing when she heard the front door open. The alarm signal jingled and the door slammed.

"Marc?"

She heard his keys hit the marble table top in the entry. "Yeah, who else would it be?"

"Why didn't you go with A.J. and Larry?" Mandy leaned over the wrought-iron balcony so she could see him.

He didn't look at her, just stomped in the direction of the kitchen. "I can't show up to work wasted, you know that."

"But A.J and Larry can?"

He lifted his shoulders before disappearing through the arch that led to the back part of the house. Mandy continued to her bedroom on soft, white carpet.

"He's such a grouch," she whispered to Scamper, scrubbing the dog's head. Then she let the fluffy ball down and started peeling off clothes, dropping them to the floor with careless abandon. She couldn't get her jeans off with her boots on, so she sat on the foot of her bed, unlaced the boots and kicked them across the room. They landed with a thud. When her socks were gone, the cool air made her wiggle her toes and sigh.

Standing, she shimmied out of her jeans and left them in a puddle. She couldn't wait to shower, wash her hair and be clean.

For some reason she was humming Rag Doll. She smiled, hearing the music in her head just as she'd heard it blasting from the truck at lunch. In the large mirror that spanned the wall of her private bathroom she looked at herself.

Good, she'd gotten some color. Her face was pink and so were her arms. It was lame that the rest of her was white as an albino. Her fair skin never tanned without a lot of coaxing. She was smart enough to slather on the sunscreen, but she wanted to have that sun kissed glow all over, not just on her arms and face. For a reason she couldn't explain, Boston's chiseled, tanned body flashed in her mind then, sending a trembling down her middle and goose bumps on her flesh.

With the shower ready, she got in and sighed under the hot pulses of water. She never took being clean and smelling fresh for granted and reveled in the nightly indulgence of a bath or long shower.

After she got out, she quickly combed through her hair, sprayed on some watermelon body splash and dressed.

Her jeans stunk. Scamper was sniffing them with the intensity of a gopher at an empty hole. Mandy wouldn't put those back on, but she knew she'd be sitting, so she chose some khaki shorts and a screened tee with 'framers nail it every time' across the chest. She'd found the shirt online, thought it was funny and bought it. Since her parents hated the shirt but happened to be gone, it was a perfect night to wear it.

Minimal makeup was her preference and she dusted some blush on her cheeks, soft shadow on her eyelids and brushed on two coats of mascara before heading downstairs.

Finished sniffing, Scamper tumbled along at her heels. The dog stopped at the top of the stairs and yipped. Mandy gathered her in her arms and carried her down the tile stairs.

Anxious to talk to Marc about the day, the job and the guys, Mandy went into the kitchen and found him hunched over a bowl of Captain Crunch. The big screen TV was on in the family room, an old episode of "Friends" playing.

"You're eating that for dinner?"

He grumbled, chewed and shrugged. Mandy put Scamper down and joined Marc at the granite counter where he sat. "I thought it went well today," she said.

Marc continued spooning and chewing.

"The guys are nice. I especially like A.J. And Larry's a total character."

Since Marc had inhaled the bowl of cereal, he poured himself some more.

"So." She shouldn't ask, sure he'd have nothing nice to say, but couldn't stop herself. "How'd I do?"

His shoulders lifted.

Mandy ignored a fluttering of insecurity she felt inside. It was Marc's way to be silent when he couldn't admit something. "I guess that means I did great." She crossed to the refrigerator and pulled out a gallon of pineapple juice, got a glass from the cupboard.

"You did what you were told, that's the main thing." Marc's mouth churned orange mush.

Mandy poured the pineapple juice. "I'm an apprentice, what else would I do?"

"As long as you remember that."

Mandy rolled her eyes and plunked the juice at his elbow. "I know you know more about this than I do. You've been at it longer. I can accept that. And I'm not asking for any special privileges you won't give the other guys."

"You won't get any." He snatched the juice, drank it all down.

"I don't expect any." Her voice rose.

"Be ready to go tomorrow or I'm leaving your butt at home and the day's over for you."

"You're still pissed Mom and Dad let me sleep in the day after grad night? I seem to remember they let you do a lot more than that after graduating. Wasn't there a trip to Cabo in there somewhere? *Un*chaperoned?"

"So." He jerked more cereal from the box and into the bowl. "This is a job, Mand, and I've got a list of guys that could take your place and carry their weight."

Mandy bristled. "I can carry my weight. I did today."

"Yeah, with A.J.'s help," Marc snorted. "Which took him from what he was doing, which slowed us down."

"You said we were going up tomorrow and we still are. To me it looks like we're still on schedule. Get over it, Marc. I'm working this job even if you hate it." Fury boiled in her veins, and she grabbed her purse so she could get out of there before the argument got uglier.

"And I do," he shouted after her.

She whirled around. "You've made that clear, what, about a thousand times now?"

"A thousand and one... and counting." He was just as furious, she could tell. He yanked the Captain Crunch box and when he did, his hand knocked into his milk-filled bowl and remnants of milk splattered out and onto the counter top. He cursed. She tried not to laugh. Before she'd taken the framing job, they both would have laughed at a moment like that. Not now. He looked ready to blow a gasket.

It was the right time for her to go upstairs and get her keys, and she did, leaving him to mutter and clean up.

chapter three

Her fisted nerves relaxed the second she opened the door of Barnes and Noble and the scent of coffee, paper and something crisp and clean she couldn't identify but wished they'd bottle and sell tickled her nose.

Mandy walked to the reading area at the back of the store at a slow and easy pace. She scanned the display tables with their stacks of books, peering down aisles, her gaze lingering on the end displays where the newest releases or series were sometimes featured.

She found Cam loitering at the end of one of four romance aisles. He still wore his black Five Buck Pizza shirt and black jeans – the business' required uniform. Why he had his backpack over his shoulder, she couldn't imagine. School had been out for two days. But the sight made her laugh.

His flame of red hair was tousled over deep green eyes and his electric smile. He leaned over, kissed her cheek. "Hey." He smelled like onions and Italian sauce.

"Hey. You're off early."

"Slow night."

"The backpack?" Mandy tugged on his strap.

"Habit. Just kidding."

"So you can hide your romance novels, I get it," she teased.

He looked around like a thief making sure he was all

clear to rip off a bank, then pulled her into the aisle. She got squeamish faced with rows and rows of book covers of buff, nearly-naked men and women with long hair blowing in the wind.

"You pick something out yet?" she asked.

His hungry gaze scanned the shelves. "Not yet. Here." He plucked a random book and thrust it at her so it would look like it was her who was looking for a romance fix.

On the cover, a buxom redhead in a shred of cloth draped strategically over her arched body was in the arms of a muscled guy with waist-length hair and wearing a loin cloth. "*Love's Savage Surrender Volume Five*?" she whispered.

"Just read it, okay?" he hissed, eyes darting.

"If anyone I knew saw me here—"

"I'm going as fast as I can. I can't just pick anything. I have taste you know."

"Mm-hmm."

"Like, no suspense. No murder stuff. I like it straight. Kidnappings I can deal with, because there's always this 'love to hate you 'cause you kidnapped me' thing going on, but other than that...Wait. Look at this. Sweet."

Mandy wasn't sure what had grabbed him about the deep red book – the color, the title or the cover, but *Prisoner of Mine* had captured him.

His eyes skimmed the back. "This sounds hot."

Mandy rolled her eyes. Her fingers itched to put the book in her hands back on the shelf. "I don't know why you read this when there are plenty of girls out there that think you're hot and you could be *living* it."

"Yeah, right," he snorted, flipping through the pages.

"If only these came illustrated."

Mandy laughed, stuck the book he'd handed her back on the shelf and tugged his sleeve. He didn't move. "You go get us seats," he muttered. "I'm going to see if I can muster up the nerve to pick out more than one."

Mandy looked around. "Aisle's all clear, you're safe." With a grin and a pat to his shoulder she left him and went in search of long-term seating.

She headed back to the open area where couches, chairs and tables were set up. A few people sat sprawled in the brown, plaid couches placed here and there for extended reading pleasure. Though meant to hold three to four customers, one guy had laid himself the length of one, his head behind a thick volume of something she couldn't read from that distance. That left only two fat, leather chairs and Mandy went right to one of the two, plopped her bag down and sat in the other. She and Cam religiously occupied a couch whenever they had a 'Barnes and Noble night' as they called them, but with mister hog-it-all stretched out like he owned the place, they'd have to use the chairs instead.

Now that she'd saved spots, she could watch people and wait, or take the risk of losing one of the places while she chose her books for the night.

If only she had something else she could leave in the chair to mark it as saved. But then she couldn't very well leave her bag. She decided people watching would have to do.

Bookstore enthusiasts intrigued her. Nowhere else, with the exception maybe of confession, could you find such a vast variety of people. Like the grey-haired man to her right. He wore his thick mane in a stubby pony tail. His black brows were pinched over black eyes, focused on a copy of *Herbs for Life*. The silky red shirt he wore buttoned to the neck made him look like he'd just stepped off the boat from the Orient.

There was a woman typing away at an open laptop. Her small glasses kept sliding to the tip of her nose, breaking her constant tapping on the keys every time she had to shove them back up.

Mandy recognized a handful of regulars who frequented the place as often as she did. The 'kissers' were one of them. The couple sat stuffed in a Lovesac, snuggling, kissing and groping, hiding behind a GQ magazine. Every week the magazine was the same, which told Mandy they weren't there for the latest in men's fashion. She let out a sigh of disapproval she hoped they heard. Neither came up for air, their lips remained locked. Disgusted, Mandy shifted, her gaze wandering back to mister hog-it-all, lying on the couch. *How rude that he still hasn't moved*, she thought, ready to storm over and rip the book out of his hands.

What could a thoughtless person like that be reading? Now that she was seated, she could read the title, *Think and Grow Rich*. She smirked. *Better to think and grow smart, buddy*. Smart as in: don't hoard all the couch space for yourself or you might end up on the floor.

"Psst. Hey."

Mandy tore her scathing gaze from mister hog-it-all to find Cam striding toward her. He had a stack of paperbacks under his arm and a look of red guilt on his face.

"You did it," she said in a congratulatory tone.

He sat down beside her, stuffing the books behind

him. "Some lady started looking in the section so I grabbed what I could. Figured I'd sort later." His darting gaze lit on the kissing couple. He eased the backpack off into the chair. "I see the kissers are here again." His gaze stayed on the couple who'd stopped to come up for air, pretending to read now.

"That's the first time they've taken a time out," Mandy whispered.

The longing was obvious in Cam's eyes. He wanted to be Mr. Kisser. "She's so amazing."

Mandy rolled her eyes. "She's taken. You will be too, when the time is right."

"You've been telling me that since junior high school." He sighed, faced her. His skin was paler than hers, a feature she knew he hated. His hair wasn't bright, but rich, almost burnt maple and it brought out the green flecks in his eyes. Through the years he'd tried dying his hair, even his eyebrows, figuring the color change would be less repugnant to girls but Mandy knew lots of girls that liked him because he was tons of fun, and he had a great face, even with the amber hair and fair skin. "I've had, what, one girlfriend in the interim?"

"Tina Margolis."

Cam nodded. "Tina Margarine everybody called her, including me. She had such greasy hair." His gaze slid back to the kissing couple. "We never did anything like that."

"Quit panting like a dog." Mandy turned his chin back toward her when his gaze started toward the lip-locked couple. "You don't have to beg for anybody."

"I don't?" He teased, grinned. "Since I can't have miss kisser over there, I'm going to drown my lust in a double chocolate mocha Italian soda." He stood. "You want anything before we settle in?"

"Yeah, get me a caramel latte freeze."

Turning, she scanned those sitting or otherwise engaged in the reading area. The woman with the laptop was still tapping away. The kissing couple was back at it, and *Herbs for Life* man was now on his second volume, *Super Herbs for Life*.

Then her gaze wandered to the guy on the couch. Only now mister hog-it-all wasn't hiding behind his *Think and Grow Rich* book. His dark brown eyes locked with hers.

Boston.

She hardly recognized him fully clothed in beaten jeans and clean white tee shirt. His explosion of dark hair wasn't mashed against his head, but thick and soft looking framing his face. Most mesmerizing were his rich, dark eyes, fastened on hers. Her pulse skipped. She waved, but all he did was slide *Think and Grow Rich* back in front of his face. Mandy frowned. Nothing intimidated her, most definitely not a guy. She took a deep breath so her pulse would settle, rose and crossed over to him.

"Hey." She stood close enough that he couldn't hide behind his book anymore, and tilted her head. "I thought maybe you didn't recognize me," she joked, "out of my construction garb."

Because he didn't sit up, didn't even open his mouth to say anything, she crossed her arms. "I know you've sworn off women, but I don't count."

She thought amusement lightened his eyes. "You're right." He sat up then, and extended long legs to the floor. "You don't count."

Her eyes bulged for only a second before slitting. "But I am the boss's daughter, and some brown nosing is absolutely mandatory."

His lips curved a little. Mandy took it as an invitation to sit down and did. "What are you doing here, anyway?"

"Aah, reading?"

"You gave up drinking and fighting off women for a night with," she tilted his book so she could read the cover, see the author's name, "Napoleon?"

He raised his arms over his head in a long stretch that lifted the hem of his tee shirt, baring ripped muscles around a blink of a bellybutton dusted with soft, dark hair. "Yeah."

Mandy's cheeks went hot when he caught her appraising him again.

"What about you?" he asked.

"Oh." She cleared her throat. "I definitely didn't want a night of drinking and fighting off women. Much rather sip an Italian soda and read. I come here all the time. I check out the house plans, stuff like that."

He glanced at her empty hands.

"I haven't gotten the books yet. I'm lucky to get a seat, so that's first priority. There isn't enough seating, but then you obviously aren't cognizant of that since you were, what, almost camped out here?"

"I like to read lying down."

"What if everybody else likes to read lying down?"

He lifted a shoulder with a playful grin. "First come, first served."

"Exactly. Not first come, first snooze."

He ticked his head at her.

At least she'd made her point about hogging the couch. "So, *Think and Grow Rich,* huh? Does it really work? It would seem to me that if it was that easy, everybody would be thinking instead of working."

"It doesn't mean you don't work. You work smarter."

"There's a smarter way to shoot a nail gun then?"

He was trying not to laugh. Mandy was glad he was still smiling.

"So you don't want to build houses all your life?" She was curious about him now, about what he protected deep inside. "What *do* you want to do?"

He shrugged but Mandy wasn't fooled by the attempt at indecision. Behind his serious eyes, his mind raced and she wanted to know with what. She opened her mouth to ask, but his eyes left hers, moving to something behind her.

Mandy turned and found Cam smiling over her shoulder. He held out the drink to her.

"Thanks." Mandy stood and took the drink. "Cam, this is Boston. He's on the framing crew I'm working with."

Cam gave a nod. Mandy watched him under tight brows wondering why he was checking out Boston with wary eyes. Boston lifted off the couch just enough so his extended hand was there for Cam to shake.

"It's Charlie," he said when they shook.

"So you work together?" Cam looked from Boston to Mandy. Mandy sipped, nodded. "Cool." Cam rocked back on his heels. "How's the job, anyway?" he addressed Mandy then, and drew from his straw. "You didn't tell me."

"It was only my first day."

"Yeah, but you've been planning this for, what, six

years?" He reached out and pinched her cheek playfully. "So was it everything you dreamed?"

She laughed. "Just about."

"Marc put up his usual stink?"

"Of course. Which he continued at home."

Cam lifted his shoulders. "Yeah, figures." He slurped again. "This is good tonight. Yours?"

"Great." Mandy realized she and Cam had gotten caught up in chatting and totally ignored Boston. She turned to him. "Well."

"Well." Cam took a step back. "I'm going to go get a...napkin. Be right back."

Mandy watched Cam go and took a long sip of the icy caramel drink.

Boston stood, and twisted his upper torso until a popping sound brought a sigh from his chest. Then he looked at Mandy. "I gotta run."

"Don't let me scare you away. I promise Cam and I will stay on the other side of the room."

His lips barely curved up. "You don't scare me." He held the book tucked next to his heart as he looked down into her eyes. *But you scare me*, she thought after a slug of want hit her in the stomach. Not because she felt like she was in harm's way. His aura was something she'd never felt before, something mysterious and alluring wrapped in two fists ready to fight. For the first time, she realized how heady it would be to have that kind of power over a guy, especially a guy sworn to resist.

"See ya tomorrow," she piped. He nodded. He walked away and Mandy followed the easy sway of his stride until he turned a corner. Her mind flashed a picture of him under the sun, bronzed and sweaty, and on his knees at her feet. She blinked, shook her head and put a cool palm over her cheek. What was with her, anyway? Why couldn't she stop thinking about Boston? Worse, she didn't have the decency to clothe him when she fantasized about him. No, he was always in his shorts and tool belt.

Priding herself on self control, Mandy looked at the couch, at the indented spot where he'd sat. "Get a hold of yourself," she muttered around her straw and sipped, but didn't taste. Then she inched toward the spot and guiltily lowered herself, sure everyone was watching. Mr. *Herbs for Life* hadn't noticed, still engrossed in his book. And the kissers were at it again, their mouths like fish under water.

"We're here now?" Cam asked coming back, napkins in hand.

"I prefer the couch, don't you?" Mandy asked.

"Yeah, I guess. I'll get the backpack. You get my books."

"Me?"

In three fast strides, Cam had the backpack and plopped himself next to her. Mandy grumbled, got up and snatched his assortment of romance novels then sat back down.

Cam settled into the couch with a dramatic shudder. "Every time I come here, the guy behind the counter in the café comes onto me."

"It's because you're so cute."

Cam winced. "I need a girlfriend, fast. One that's female preferably." Cam looked around. "Speaking of... where's your friend?"

"He's hardly my friend. We work together."

"That generally makes people friends."

"Not with this guy," she mumbled. "He's sworn off females."

Cam's face twisted. "I knew there was something wrong with him."

"You did not. He's just—"

"Believe me, I speak from experience. Only, I'm not stupid enough to self impose such a torturous state of being. That gives self-flagellation a new name. What, don't tell me—he's gay."

"Of course not." Why she felt compelled to defend Boston, baffled her. "He got burned. At least that's what the guys tell me."

"The guys?"

"The other guys on the framing team."

Cam nodded. "They masochistic like he is?"

She shook her head and sucked the last bit of her drink until air scraped the straw. "They're red-blooded and horny like you."

Cam buried his face in his hands. "See? It's just something you girls will never understand, this drive, this need, this thing so big—"

"Stop! Stop!" Mandy laughed, shoving one of his books at him. "Here."

"No, I'm serious. Girls never—"

"One of the sexes has to maintain control, Cameron. God made sure he gave the extra power to women that's all."

Cam groaned, and his gaze went back to the kissing couple. "Like you don't have enough power over us already."

"You got that." Mandy shook her empty cup, rattling

ice and the straw. Another vision of Boston on his knees at her feet flashed through her head. She tipped back her cup for the last drop of drink, determined not to think of him again.

chapter four

The next morning, Mandy stood with the guys in a semi-circle around Marc, waiting for her assignment as they started work framing the second floor.

"Charlie and me will work the family room. A.J., you and Larry start in the office and bath." Marc slid a hard stare at Mandy. "You can nail."

Mandy crossed her arms. "That's flunkie work."

Marc gave a cocky shrug. He smiled at Boston, jerked his head, and the two of them started off to the other side of the house.

Mandy ground out a growl. It wasn't professional to argue with the boss, even if the boss was her brother, someone she'd spent plenty of time arguing with. Like an obedient apprentice, she kept her mouth zipped. She took in a deep breath.

"He just doesn't want you to get hurt." A.J. was already at the six foot stack of joists with a grin on his face. He had his head wrapped again, this time with a blue bandana, and he looked like a pirate.

"He's such a chauvinist," Mandy mumbled. She pulled out her hammer and gave it a swing in Marc's direction.

A.J. and Larry lifted a stack of two-by-ten foot joists and carried them closer to the area where they would be working.

"He could care less about me getting hurt. He just doesn't want me doing anything that will make me his equal."

A.J. crossed back to the waiting stack of lumber with a grin aimed at her. "You're already his equal." He bent over, ready to pick up another piece, and waited until Larry had gripped it. "One, two, three." He walked backwards, leading Larry to the spot where they dropped the wood into a pile.

Begrudgingly, Mandy started at one corner of the house and double checked the plywood sheathing for secure placement. Every now and then she shot Marc a glare, even though he was engrossed in work and didn't see.

It took most of the morning to lay the floor joists over the main floor. Mandy envied Boston and Larry lithely balancing on the installed beams overhead like tightrope walkers in a circus. Once there were enough joists, plywood flooring was laid on top, creating a growing floor of wood.

"How's the nailing coming there Mand?" Marc stood smiling down at her.

Mandy rolled her eyes upward, her expression grouchy. "Super." Basically, she'd had nothing to do. The structure was solid as a fortress. At least Marc was doing a good job overseeing quality. Her dad would be happy about that.

Because she was on her own, she listened to the pairs talk.

"Another dollar in the pot," A.J. laughed, shaking his head at Larry. The two of them were creating their own spreading platform of flooring that would meet Marc and Boston's in the center before lunch break, Mandy estimated.

"What?" Marc stopped. "Another woman?"

All work ceased as every gaze shifted to Larry whose lazy grin spread wide when he lifted his shoulders.

"You're an animal," Marc's voice cracked with disbelief.

"She was something else, too." Larry's legs hung down from the joists he was straddling. "A real livewire."

"Man, how do you find 'em? I've never seen a guy with your luck." Marc shook his head and hammered. "And the variety..."

"Yeah, well, I prefer a buffet to one dish."

"Most of us would." Marc moved positions and helped Boston fit another piece of plywood into place. "Every time I hook up with a woman I say to myself, is this really what I want when there's so much out there?" Mandy snorted out a laugh and Marc glared down at her. "What?"

"You're miserable when you don't have somebody and you moan and groan when you do. I think that's your answer right there."

"I am not miserable."

"I live with you." Mandy stood underneath where the floor above was gradually coming together and looked up into Marc's scowl. "You're worse than a premenstrual woman, and you're not just lame for a few days of the month, either."

The guys laughed, but Marc tilted his head at her. Mandy enjoyed putting him on the spot. "You should go with Larry. Maybe you'll pick up some tips."

"I can pick up my own women," Marc bit out.

"I work alone, man." Finished with the center joists, Larry swung his legs up and stood. Then he jumped over on the landing where A.J. was working.

Mandy tapped her chin. "What about you, A.J.? Would you be willing to drag along your boss one night for some on-the-spot tutoring? He might be willing to give you a promotion since that would qualify as some pretty good brown-nosing."

"Zip it up, Mandy," Marc's voice was hard, his gaze harder staring down at her.

A.J.'s eyes twinkled. Mandy could tell he was enjoying this discussion as much as she was. "Sure, I could take you along, boss, since we go for different types."

This interested Mandy more than ribbing her brother, and she turned and looked up at A.J. "So what type do you go for, A.J.? No, let me guess."

"This should be interesting," Marc teased, resuming his hammering.

A.J. paused and looked at her in a way that sent something warm but unidentifiable through her.

"She'd be sporty, into dirt biking, mountain climbing, wind surfing, stuff like that. I'm guessing she'd be tall and tan – so you guys would match. Hmm. Blonde or brunette..." Mandy liked the way he blinked slow and lazy as if he was thinking about what she was saying. "You'd appreciate either, being raised with sisters. But she'd be attractive for sure. Not beautiful or exotic, more cute or pretty. Am I right?"

Amusement kept his smile wide. He reached into his nail sack and took out a nail. "A gentleman never talks about other women around a lady." Holding the nail in place, he gave it one, fast whack.

"Guess I'm not a gentleman then," Marc laughed.

Larry joined him. "Me either. Heck, I get my best inside info from women."

"So that's how you do it," Marc said.

"Part of how." Larry ripped his shirt off and swiped the sweat from his face, then under his arms and across his chest. "The other part's my willing body."

"So another dollar goes into the pot?" Mandy shaded her eyes from the sun, now making an arc in the middle of the sky bringing along sweltering temperatures. "Do you even know this girl's name?"

Larry bunched his tee shirt between his hands and thought a moment. The guys laughed when he couldn't come up with her name. "Hey, catch this, will ya?" Larry tossed down his damp shirt before Mandy had the chance to say, *forget it*.

"Mine too." Marc's came flying at her next, and hit her in the face. She scowled at him, peeling it off of her head.

"Excuse me?" she said, holding both shirts at arms' length in her fingertips.

When Boston pulled his shirt up over his head, she took an involuntary breath. The muscles under his skin rippled under his smooth, tanned skin. She tossed Larry and Marc's shirts into a nearby corner. "Um, I can take that," she offered with a shrug. Boston looked at her for a long moment. She held her hands up and he dropped the shirt down. For a second she fantasized about bringing the warm garment to her nose and taking a deep breath. But that would look utterly strange, so she stuffed the shirt into her crooked arm before bending to snatch up the others.

"It's totally unfair that you guys get all over tans and I'm stuck with a construction tan."

"Baby doll." A.J.'s voice had her turning. He stood shirtless too, and smiling. "Will you put mine with theirs?"

"Sure."

His shirt came at her like velvet on a breeze, and she grabbed it mid air, then curtseyed for them. "Anything else? I'm just ye old slave girl here."

"Yeah," Marc laughed. "Get us some water."

Mandy shook her head. "One minute I'm a flunkie, the next I'm a laundress," her tone was dry with sarcasm. "Get your own water." She took the shirts to a clean corner of the house and dropped them. She was about to leave them there but heard Boston.

"Uh, would you…could you fold mine, please?"

Mandy stopped dead in her tracks and looked up at him. So what if he looked like some golden god up there, giving out commands. "Fold?" she asked.

"Mandy doesn't fold," Marc said. "You should see her room. Does it even have a floor? I haven't seen one in about five years."

"If it's folded it won't be wrinkled when I put it back on." Boston looked adorably embarrassed to be asking, so Mandy tilted her head back and forth for a minute as if she was trying to decide.

"Okay." She squatted down and folded all of the shirts. "At least I know *how* to fold. That's more than I can say for you, Marcus." After she'd finished, she picked up her hammer and crossed back to the corner she'd already checked twice for secure fittings. "Gee, maybe if you'd give me something else to do, I wouldn't be folding."

"Fine. Start sweeping up."

Mandy's eyes bulged. "We're not even halfway through the day. That's clean up work."

Marc lifted his shoulders. "You wanted something to do."

Mandy's eyes slit. He wanted to play mean? She dug out her cell phone with a smile just as mean as she felt. He shook his head. Mandy spoke into her phone, even though she hadn't really dialed. She made sure her tone teased. "Daddy?"

"All right, fine. Fine." Marc climbed down one of the ladders looking ready to growl.

"Play fair," she told him.

He brought his face to hers. "Fair would be you at home, baking cookies and reading books, or going to college somewhere very far away."

That hurt, and he hadn't even whispered it. Mandy wanted to slap him. Instead, she lifted her chin and tucked the phone back in her belt.

"Lunch!" Marc boomed, sending Mandy back a step. He bowled over to the truck without saying another word, unbuckling his tool belt.

The guys seemed to drop from the sky, and soon they were all heading toward the truck.

Joining them, Mandy waited, trying not to feel crushed under Marc's work boot. It was so unfair, not to mention unprofessional, that he bullied her in front of them.

But it wasn't her way to dwell on something unpleasant. That only made you more miserable. She decided instead to enjoy the sight of Boston's bare, lean back. He was standing right in front of her and with every move as he unbuckled and then lifted the belt to put it away, a glorious masterpiece of movement shifted underneath his flawless skin. Her stomach growled, bringing all heads around to her.

She lifted her shoulders in a coy shrug, then stepped in between the guys unhooking her belt. "Today, I pick lunch."

"No way," Marc snapped.

"Sorry, my pick today Marc." Mandy set her belt in the box with the others, then stepped back so each of them could reach over and grab a shirt from the pile. "It's only fair."

"She's right." A.J.'s grin winked to her right. He ripped off his bandana, rubbed his hair until it stood up like a porcupine, then tucked the swatch of fabric in his back pocket.

"I don't care one way or the other." Larry shrugged into a Haynes shirt he'd grabbed from the back of the truck and climbed into the truck bed, making himself comfortable.

"What about you, Boston?" Mandy looked at him and he turned, his dark eyes unreadable but magnetic. Mandy's heart skipped. "What would Napoleon say?"

His smile was even more beautiful than she'd imagined with white teeth that gleamed off his tanned skin. Mandy was sure she'd finally broken through his austere barrier. "He'd say it isn't smart for an employee to interfere with his boss's decision, especially if it's something as basic as lunch."

"A lame answer." She hooked her arm in A.J.'s and lifted her chin. "A.J. sides with me, so the vote swings in my favor."

Marc slammed on the breaks. "No way." The big truck idled in front of Barnes and Noble bookstore. "What are we supposed to eat? Paper?"

"They have a café inside." Mandy was sitting next to him with A.J. on her right. She shoved her left foot over, kicked his aside and pressed on the gas pedal. He let out a screech as the truck lurched forward.

"A café? For what? Crumpets? Tarts? I want food."

"Pull in and stop being a baby."

With a muttered curse, Marc yanked the truck into a spot. "An appetizer, that's what this place is." He threw open the door and hopped out. Mandy thought it'd be safer to go out A.J.'s door. He was wearing a grin, and didn't look like he wanted to kill her.

Boston and Larry jumped over the truck bed. Larry squinted up at the sign. "It's a bookstore."

Mandy started toward the entrance. "Might as well refine ourselves while we eat." They were trailing her, albeit warily. She worked to keep the grin off her face.

"Refine ourselves?" Larry mumbled, scratching his crotch.

"When I eat, I eat," Marc grumbled. They were at the doors. "I can't eat and do something else at the same time."

A.J. pulled the door open and gestured for Mandy to enter and she did. "I know *you* can't," she tossed over her shoulder. "But that doesn't mean the rest of us won't enjoy a nice meal while browsing over a book or a magazine."

"Whatever," Marc sneered, air from inside the store gusting wafts of brewing coffee in his face.

"I don't know." Larry looked around now that they were inside. "This doesn't feel right. Like hooking up and getting your teeth cleaned at the same time. The two just don't mix, you know?"

"That's what I've been saying," Marc concurred.

Mandy took a right, through magazines and straight to the café. First she eyed the rich and gooey desserts in the glassed-in display. *Mmm. Oreo cheesecake.* But the mud brownie looked awfully good, too.

"May I help you?" A guy with black hair molded into a baby mowhawk on the top of his head addressed her.

Only A.J. stood next to her, the other guys were approaching with the hesitancy of being burned at the stake. Even Boston. *What was this, "I've never been in this place before" look?* She knew better than to bring up that she'd seen him here, so she turned and ordered. "I'll take a hot muffelatta, a bag of Sunchips, a piece of Oreo cheesecake and a Pepsi."

A.J.'s grin widened with approval. Since the waiter was waiting, he ordered next.

Mandy moved aside to wait for her meal. She didn't want to miss seeing what the guys would order. A.J. picked a ham and cheese bagel, a Coke and chips. Larry stood, arms crossed, face twisted, staring at the menu. He waved Marc ahead.

Marc grunted at Mandy. "What're you having, Mand?"

"A hot muffelatta."

"A hot whatta? What the?"

"It's good, you'll like it. Promise. They're New

Orleans' famous."

"Oh." Marc's expression brightened, "That's cool then. I'll take one of those muff things." Marc pulled out his money.

Boston stepped up and ordered a vegetarian sandwich in a pita, no mayo, no chips and water. Mandy tilted her head. Decidedly a health nut, but then, that body of his pretty much defined an organically perfect male.

She wondered what, if any, reading material he would choose to enjoy over lunch, doubting he'd bring Napoleon to the table with the guys around. Since her meal wasn't ready, she took a peek at the magazines, grabbed the latest *Architectural Digest, Southern Home Builders* and *Homes Today* then found two tables and slid them together.

A.J. approached with both of their lunches and a smile when he saw her moving the tables. He set down the plates. "Good choice, baby doll."

"Thank you." She dipped in a quick curtsey, pulled out a chair and sat, propping the magazines to the left of her plate. A.J. pulled out the chair across from her, eyeing her choice of reading material. Then he set off for the magazine racks.

Marc and Larry stood grumbling over by the napkin/straw/utensil stand. Order in hand, Boston was on his way to the table. Mandy tried not to enjoy the delicious heat drizzling through her. He reminded her of a black panther when he walked. She couldn't stop looking at him.

She patted the empty spot next to her. "Here. Remember, I don't count."

He hesitated only a moment then took the

seat. Mandy was glad they were alone. "No reading material?" she queried.

He reached for his water. "I don't eat and read." He drank, set the glass down.

"Like Larry?"

"Nothing like Larry." His long fingers deftly wrapped around the pita and he lifted it to his mouth. "But it was a nice idea, bringing us here." His brown eyes sparkled for a second. Mandy blinked, sure she imagined it.

"You like your literature straight then." She plucked a chip, popped it in her mouth. "I take it either way – *any* way, actually. I can always read, and I can always eat." She flashed a smile that she noted he caught, watched.

"So I've noticed."

"You got a problem with a girl that has an appetite?"

He looked ready to laugh, but didn't. "No."

"You like your food as straight as your literature," she went on, because she had his attention. "Healthy. Clean."

He smiled, turning a shade darker with a blush.

"What?" she ribbed him. "It's true. Salad yesterday, vegetarian pita today."

"And you eat like a garbage disposal." His gaze skimmed her meal.

Marc and Larry ambled over but Mandy wasn't about to let the conversation she had going with Boston get lost in a bunch of male grumbling. "Excuse me? Garbage disposal?" She crunched another Sunchip.

"Look at this." Boston waved a hand over her food. "And it was even worse yesterday."

"What was worse?" Marc pulled out a chair with his

foot and sat.

Boston swallowed a bite. "What she eats."

"I told you she eats like a pig." Marc stared at his mile high muffelatta and let out a sigh. "How do you pick this thing up? Do I start in the middle or on the ends?"

Mandy rolled her eyes. "Hard to believe he can read a blueprint, isn't it?"

A.J. came back with *Esquire* under his arm. Larry stole a look at the cover, then grabbed an extra chair and brought it to a corner of the table. "No *For Men Only*?" he asked.

"Ew," Mandy shuddered. "Not over lunch. Please."

"Now we're talking." Marc piped, then slugged fists with Larry across the table.

A.J. sat, spread the magazine open on his thigh, and reached for his sandwich, settling in.

"What're these?" Marc held his sandwich poised and ready, was eyeing the greenery poking out of the sandwich. "Green thingies."

"Green olives," Mandy said. "They're good for you. Eat them." To her right, Boston let out a laugh. "What?"

"This coming from you?" He reached over, and when he did, his shoulder pressed heat into her arm. He lifted the top of her sandwich.

"I've got plenty of greenery," she tossed back. "There's olives in here – green olives. See?"

When he chewed, the bones in his jaw pressed against tan, taut skin. Mandy now knew it was possible to look totally hot while eating. She could tell he didn't agree with her about greenery and health, but was cool with her opinion. Marc's cheeks were stuffed like a hamster's, the edges of his muffelatta gone. Larry was halfway through a personal pan quiche and A.J. had finished his ham and cheese and was deep into his magazine.

"Only problem with this place," Marc's mouth moved the food inside like an open washing machine, "there's not enough." After stuffing the last piece in, his gaze latched on Mandy's plate.

She made a grab for it too late. He snagged the second half of her muffelatta with a wicked grin.

"Hey!"

His mouth closed over the sandwich like a raptor's. Mandy picked up a chip and threw it at him. "What?" he complained. "You still have a piece of cheesecake." With another bite, the muffelatta disappeared. "In fact," he sputtered between chews, "don't mind if I do."

Mandy slapped his hand back and held the slice of cheesecake out of his reach. "I need energy."

"For what?" Marc choked out a laugh. "It doesn't take much to shoot a nail gun."

"I've secured the whole main floor," she protested. "When we get back, I'm going up." Fork poised to cut into the creamy cheesecake she pointed the tines at him. "I am."

Marc threw back the last of his drink. "My breath's gonna stink now after that thing." He made a face at her. "I have a social life to consider. Nobody's gonna get near me after the onions and salami I just ate."

"They wouldn't get near you anyway," she bit out, still simmering. Boston was trying not to look like he was listening to their petty argument. A.J. was too engrossed in *Esquire* to notice and Larry was, as always, clueless.

"So we on for later?" Marc crumpled his napkin into

a ball and tossed it at Larry to get his attention. "You, me?"

Larry picked up his now empty plate and licked it. Even Marc's eyes bulged. Boston looked itchy from the inside out and shook his head. Mandy almost laughed.

"Liked that, eh, Lar?" Mandy asked.

"Pretty good." Larry set the plate down. "I never had quiche before."

"Now you're a real man," Mandy teased. "You can use it for your opening line tonight. 'Hey, I'm Larry and I eat quiche. Wanna dance?'"

Larry shrugged then leaned back in the chair, both arms out in a stretch that almost broke his face in two. "Don't dance, so that'd be impossible."

"Oh, but you eat quiche? Cool guys dance." Mandy speared her last bite of cheesecake. "Girls like that."

"I'm not into girls." Larry leaned forward, plunked his elbows on the table and shook out his hair like a wet dog shakes off water. "I'm into women."

Mandy rolled her eyes as she chewed the last bite of cheesecake.

"You've never seen anything like it, swear." There was awe in Marc's voice. "The guy just baits em, hooks 'em and plops em right into the frying pan."

Mandy scowled. "You're a dork comparing women to a meal."

"Might as well," Larry's laugh was wicked. "The way I—"

"Don't even go there." Mandy held up a hand and closed her eyes on a shudder.

Marc landed a hard pat to Larry's shoulder. "That's why I'm watching." He pointed to Larry. "Teacher." Then pointed to himself. "Student."

"I'm not sure you should watch him do anything, now that I know he doesn't dance." Mandy reached for her Pepsi.

"I only dance in the sheets," Larry grinned.

"The only place that counts." Marc lifted his fist and met Larry's.

"Don't you guys ever think about anything else?" Mandy made her disgust obvious in her tone. Marc and Larry looked at each other.

"No." They said the word in unison, then laughed. Mandy glanced at Boston for a read. He looked embarrassed and ready to flee. At least he wasn't agreeing with these two.

"We ready to go now?" Boston was clearly trying to change the subject.

"You guys have to stop talking like that, you're making Boston uncomfortable." She placed her hand on his shoulder. "Have some respect for our resident monk." She waited for his eyes to meet hers.

When they did, something flickered—warning, want—she wasn't sure, but the corner of his jaw twitched, and he glanced at where she touched him. Her hand melted away, somehow made it to her lap. She wasn't aware of the electric silence now at the table, too fixed on his face. On trying to figure out what he was thinking. Suddenly, she felt like she was under a microscope. One sweep around the table and she found everybody watching. Even A.J., his green eyes locked her from over the top the Esquire magazine.

"New bet," Marc announced, eyes bright with mischief.

Mandy straightened, flustered. To her right, Boston hadn't moved, like her touch had turned him into a statue. "Yeah?" her voice cracked. "What's that?"

"Bucks on how long Boston stays celibate." Marc dug out his wallet.

Boston sat forward, shaking his head. His hands, Mandy noted, those gorgeous long fingers, shook even though he was trying to hide them in a clasp. "No. No way."

"Why not?" Larry pulled out a wad of bills held together with a paperclip.

"Because I'm not...I don't want—"

"Course you don't. That's what I'm betting on, man." Marc pulled out a five dollar bill. Larry whistled. "We each pick the number of days we think it'll take before Charlie here breaks. Winner gets the pot when he does."

"I'm in," Larry said. "I've seen this guy. He's...I don't know what he is, superman or something. Nobody's gonna crack the wall around that guy's libido."

"Guys," Boston's voice had a thread of pleading that wound hot and fast through Mandy's system. "Forget it."

"Don't think you can do it?" Mandy taunted Boston. She couldn't help it, he was adorable vulnerable. So cute, dipping his head, tapping his fingers, shifting in that seat as if he had a cockroach in his boxers. And those eyes, frustrated when they slid over to hers. *Aw.* She wanted to pat his cheek and tell him everything was going to be just fine.

"I can do it." His black-hot eyes held hers.

"Sure you can." Smiling, A.J. set down his magazine

and reached into his back pocket for his wallet.

"No temptations now, guys," Mandy chided. A.J. took out a dollar. "You have to play fair."

"Course we will," Marc's teeth flashed. "Just like we always do."

For a moment Boston hid behind his hands. He shook his head, let out a groan. "I'm not going to any bars or clubs," he said, dragging his hands down his face. "And none of your crap, Larry."

"Course not." Marc's brows wagged. "We'll just let nature take its course. A.J., you be the keeper of the bets and the cash." He grabbed four napkins, pulled a pen out of his back pocket and wrote on it before folding it and handing it to A.J. Then he handed out the remaining napkins to Larry, A.J. and Mandy. "Aren't you in, Mand?"

Mandy bit her lower lip. Four pairs of eyes locked on her all at once. *What's a girl to do?* She looked at Boston. What was that expression? Curiosity. Daring. Mortification. And something else, like if she put her money on the bet, it'd be over. Only she wasn't sure what *it* was.

She snatched the napkin out of Marc's hand and dug through her purse for a pen.

chapter five

The guys were spread out, securing the last sections of plywood flooring on the second floor. Mandy had no intention of staying below shooting off nails one more minute. Since they'd be starting to erect the walls soon, she carried six-by-fours up to the second level and laid them out so they'd be ready.

Larry had brought a boombox and it sat blasting hard rock. The band was crass, raunchy and too loud, but Mandy knew better than to say something. Apprentices had to keep their mouths shut about incidentals or they'd find themselves off the job.

Still, she wished she'd brought her iPod.

After her tenth haul toting the long pieces of wood over her left shoulder, her body started to weep. Only A.J. and Boston had bothered looking over every now and then at her, she'd seen their heads turn out the corner of her eye but didn't acknowledge them, too afraid of appearing like she was looking for help.

Sweat beaded along her forehead, dribbled down her spine and her chest. How she wished she could rip off her shirt and jeans so there was nothing between her and the air but her underwear. She hoisted a four-by-six over her shoulder and headed up again.

Once they'd gotten back from lunch, the guys had stripped down to the bare minimum: shorts and tool belts. Their muscles shifted and gleamed under the hot afternoon sun. Mandy's throat was parched just looking at the lot of them: bronzed backs, chests, arms and legs reaching, bending, lifting – working to the limit.

The piece of wood fell from her shoulder to the floor in a thud. So caught up in the tanned vision of masculinity in movement, she didn't take into account that the pieces might topple and roll until too late. The wood tumbled onto her toes.

"Ouch!" She hopped back, favoring the injured foot. Flushed, she limped away, cursing beneath her breath that she'd been distracted and stupid.

"You okay there, baby doll?"

Both A.J. and Boston stopped and were looking over. She waved. "Yeah, fine. Thanks."

Just what I don't need, she thought, starting back down the makeshift stairs. For Marc to have any excuse to fire her. *She's not strong enough, not tough enough, not capable*. Frustration had her hauling two pieces this time. Her jeans stuck to her legs, her bangs to her forehead. Air puffed in and out of her chest as she climbed the stairs, balancing the long planks. Underneath her leather gloves, her palms were soaked.

This time she let out a furious groan and tossed the wood like a javelin into the already existing pile. Seething, she stood frozen a moment. After that growl, they'd all stopped, and now they were staring at her. Sweat dripped in her eyes, burned and ran in streams down her arms and neck. Breath heaved in and out like she'd just run a marathon. They wanted tough? She'd show them tough.

Marc's lips curled. "Glad to see you're finally

working."

She bared her teeth at him, fingers curling. How she'd love to have aimed that throw at his gut and knocked him over. Larry let out a snicker and went back to work. *Make that two*, Mandy thought, fantasizing about spearing a piece at Larry as well. A.J.'s green eyes were sharp, glancing at Marc before turning back to her. "You need a hand, you let me know, baby doll."

"No hand needed, but thanks, A.J." Mandy swiped her forehead.

A.J. hammered in the final piece of flooring.

Boston's dark eyes seemed to simmer, his body was tight as if he was ready to pounce on Marc. The sight sucked the anger right out of Mandy, replacing it with a fast bolt of admiration. She couldn't enjoy it, not in front of Marc, but she wanted Boston to know she appreciated him siding with her, even if he did it silently.

She gave him a sharp nod, turned and headed back downstairs. Her muscles quivered. Rock music pounded through the structure, shaking the house frame with the beat. Brash, hard lyrics and screaming guitar licks drove more frustration through her, but the image of Boston, steaming and powerful standing there ready to rip into Marc created a delicious craving low inside of her that intensified with every pound of the drum.

Her mind rolled images of him on his knees at her feet, his crown of dark hair glistening in the sun. Then his face tipped up and his black eyes locked on hers in that way that turned her legs to noodles.

Wood. Dirt. Sweat. The scents mixed, heated and created an intoxicating elixir. She reached for three more pieces of wood and set them on her shoulder just as another image flashed: Her back pressed into the framed wall and Boston coming for her, the tools in his belt clinking, the sweat on his body shimmering through that panther walk of his.

She had to stop this. *Climb*, she told herself, taking the stairs up. Desire swam like a thousand currents out of control in her blood. He was back at work, thankfully. She'd probably have plunged a foot through the makeshift stairs if he'd been watching her.

Are you kidding yourself? He's not going to watch you with that bet going on. Now, more than ever, he'd be distant, bent on proving he could withstand anything even remotely feminine.

Mandy dropped the wood in the pile and chewed her lip. He had his back to her, bent over as he crouched down with A.J., the two of them fitting and hammering. The long curve of his spine was quite lovely, she thought, admiring the soft, ridged bones of ribs veiled by strong muscle. What was wrong with her? She knew anatomy. So why was every detail of the male body suddenly very apparent? She was ashamed that she couldn't just look—she was staring.

Perturbed, she climbed back down the stairs and headed for her water bottle. The temperature was reaching beyond ninety-five. Mix that with her over-zealous libido and it might as well be one hundred and twenty degrees. Something had to give.

After guzzling half the bottle, she let out an, "Ah," lifted the hem of her tee shirt and swiped her face. She didn't care about exposing her stomach and bra, the guys were still upstairs. Tomorrow she'd bring a towel, she decided, moving the blue tee shirt down her face nice and slow so she every last bit of sweat was gone. Then she opened her eyes.

Boston stood at the base of the stairs.

Her heart tapped against her ribs. She pulled her tee shirt into place. As if it didn't matter that he'd come down and caught her with her shirt up, she took another drink from the water bottle.

When he neared, his sweat and scent overtook hers. Masculine devoured feminine. Mandy licked her lips. He bent over, grabbed his water bottle from the cooler and twisted off the lid, his brown eyes locked on hers.

"You okay?" he asked.

Her insides trembled along with her overworked muscles. "Fine." She tilted her head back to drink what was left in her bottle, mortified when nothing came.

The corners of his mouth turned up just enough to cause her to blush. He held out his icy bottle to her. She shook her head. He drank, and her eyes widened watching the rhythmic up and down motion of his throat as he consumed the water. He closed his eyes, bliss, satisfaction, and pleasure on his face.

Mandy blinked and found his dark gaze once again with hers. He wiped his mouth with the back of his hand. "It's good that you stand up for yourself."

"I always stand up for myself," she said.

"I can tell that about you." He tilted his head back in another long drink, and again she watched his tanned throat shift. A flash of dark hair peeked out from underneath his lifted armpit, and she bit her lip.

"Your brother needs some lessons in how to treat women."

Mandy smiled. "I don't think I count in his book."

He twisted the lid back on the bottle. "Sister or not, he needs some lessons."

"For Marc, the playing field is even at work. If I want my own crew someday, I have to be willing and able to do it all."

"You really want to work on site?"

"I wouldn't be here if I didn't. So," she started, ready to change the subject. "Did your old girlfriend stand up for herself? Or was she a wimp?"

He let out a sharp grunt and screwed the lid back on the water bottle. "Wimp."

"Ah." Mandy nodded.

He leaned over and put the nearly-empty bottle back inside the cooler. "I'm not the wimp type." Then he stood upright, hands on his hips, gaze meeting hers. "But I've been stupid."

"Not stupid," she corrected, hating that he would think so about himself. "Blinded maybe."

He lifted a shoulder. "Maybe."

"It's okay as long as you learned something from it, and I don't mean being extreme and abstaining from all females because that's the easy way around it."

His eyes narrowed some. "You think it's easy?"

"Ignoring's easy. Conquering is something else."

His tongue wet his lips. He studied her and didn't say anything for what seemed like endless minutes. Mandy hoped she hadn't been too bold, but she never tailored her words to fit guys.

"You have a boyfriend?" he asked.

"Not currently."

"But you've had one."

"Sure," she shrugged. They'd been short little flings,

the longest lasted about a month, but they counted.

"Any of the guys start out one way and morph into something else?"

There was bite in his tone. Old anger. "No. Not really."

"Then you were smarter than me." His hands slipped to his sides, a look of hurt and defeat passed over his face. Mandy had the urge to reach out and touch his cheek and tell him everything was going to be all right.

"Girls can be two-faced." She was mad at whoever had hurt him. "Manipulating witches," she went on, voice rising. "We're not all that way. I hope you—"She stopped herself. What she wanted was for him to heal and give women another chance. Give *her* a chance. But those thoughts remained safely tucked away. The look in his eyes was guarded, as if they stood on opposite sides of a raging river and she held the only rope. She wondered if she threw it to him, would he catch it and hold on or let it fall into the river.

He let out a breath. "That's why I'm taking a break from women."

Mandy swallowed a thick knot. He sounded so resigned. Rather than try to talk him out of it, she nodded. "Good thinking."

She looked around for a trash box because she needed to throw away the empty water bottle, but also because she didn't want him to see disappointment on her face. It was obvious he was set on this course of abstinence.

Random boxes could be found all over a construction site, and she found the nearest one and tossed her empty bottle into it, a pitch of frustration behind it. Did he have to be so determined? Couldn't he be weak like every other male on the planet and give into the basic animal inside?

She looked at him again. He stood watching, as if waiting. For what, she wasn't sure. She swallowed. His vow was going to be a lot harder on her than on him.

"Hey you two," Marc called. Both of their heads snapped around to the stairs. Marc was halfway down, dipping so he could see them. A big grin spread on his face. Mandy flushed and glanced at Boston who scratched the back of his head before starting back over to the stairs.

"I was just getting a drink." Boston took the stairs up.

"No problem," Marc's grin deepened. "You're entitled."

Mandy watched Boston's tanned, muscled legs until they vanished upstairs. She let out a sigh. Looking pleased as the Cheshire cat Marc wagged his brows at her then disappeared to the second level. Suspicion socked her in the stomach. Nobody looked that happy without a reason. What was Marc up to?

• • • • •

By late afternoon they had one quarter of the second floor exterior walls framed. The baking sun inched down the westerly sky with no breeze to cut the air, ripening with the smell of sweat and dirt and wood.

Mandy held a four-by-six in place while A.J secured the base of it. Larry's rock music was still pounding, as if competing with the hammers and nail guns. Her temples started to throb.

"Could we change the music?" she called over her shoulder. "I think we've listened to this, what, about fifty times now? I've got a headache."

"Don't have anything else," Larry hollered back. "Side's it's mood music."

Mandy looked over where he and Marc mirrored what she and A.J. were doing. Larry said something to Marc, scratched his butt crack and let out a laugh. Mandy shook her head. "I don't even want to think about what those two are discussing."

With each of A.J.'s hammer, pounds vibrated through her hands and arms.

"Yup. Sweet little thing like you shouldn't even know about stuff like that."

Mandy looked down at A.J. crouched at her feet, the red bandana on his head wrapped tight over his caramel hair, and thought of her Boston fantasy. A.J. wasn't on his knees, but he was at her feet, securing the post. His back was thicker with muscles than Boston's, but just as smooth. His shoulders, wide and powerful, bunched and eased with every movement. A tiny red flower was tattooed on his left deltoid.

"Nice tattoo."

A.J. let out a laugh-grunt. "Not sure how nice it is."

"It's a flower. At least it's not something obnoxious. When did you get it?"

"After high school." One more hard slam of the hammer and he stood. She hadn't noticed how close they were working because he'd been down at her feet. Now, his chest was inches from hers. His green eyes crinkled into a grin.

She took a deep breath, filling her senses with his

sweat, the natural scent of his skin and the comforting smells of the site.

He lifted his arm, and looked at the tattoo. "A mistake."

"Must have been a girl," she said.

He considered her answer and his eyes sharpened. "A woman, yeah."

Mandy was intrigued by the mysterious tattoo and the story. When he moved to pick up another four-by-six, she stayed on his tail. "So, what happened?"

He carried the piece over to the inside wall they were constructing and they fitted it into place. "She wanted it to remind me of her."

"That's not altogether unreasonable." Mandy held the piece in place while he dug into his belt for nails. The smile he normally wore slipped away.

"Not for her." His eyes slit some. "But the relationship didn't last, and now I have the tattoo forever." He dropped down and started hammering. His biceps bulged like fists ready to strike. The little flower stretched and swayed with the movement of his skin.

"Did you love her?" Mandy almost slapped herself. Why would she ask such a question?

He didn't even break rhythm hammering. "Thought I did."

"Why else would you brand yourself?" she murmured.

He looked up, his eyes a flickering puzzle in green and gold. He stood again, staying close. "Branding." A low chuckle slid from his lips. Wide, firm lips, Mandy noticed, over brilliant white teeth. "You women can get us to do anything you want, you know that don't you?"

He reached up and hammered the top of the piece into place.

Her body suddenly filled with a thousand fireflies, scrambling for a way out. "Hold it steady there." His voice was kind, even though she knew very well she'd lost her grip. She couldn't help it. He was so close, she felt so small and...female.

"Sorry," she muttered, shuddering.

"No problem." He glanced over. "You cold, baby doll?"

"No." But she shuddered again.

She and A.J. finished by the time the sun finally slid behind the low, western mountain range, throwing purple-orange shadows out in blessed streams that cooled the air. Because Marc and Larry had plans, they'd finished earlier and now waited by the truck in their red *Haynes* shirts. Their laughter bounced through the framed rooms. Boston, Mandy noticed, had worked solo most of the afternoon, slowly framing in a section across from where she and A.J. had spent the day.

"Let's hustle up!" Marc called from the truck.

"Almost done, boss." A.J. wore a wide grin as he placed the last four-by-six into place. Mandy held the wood firm. "So, is it just you and Marc?" he asked, squatting down to hammer.

"Just us. What about you? You said you had sisters, right?"

A.J. hammered. "Four."

"That explains why you know women so well."

A.J. chuckled. "You'd think, but sometimes I'm no smarter than the next guy."

"Women and sisters are a different breed," Mandy said, and casually looked across at Boston. He had to hear their conversation. The music was over, thankfully, and he was too close not to catch what they were saying even if he did appear to be politely ignoring it. "I'm amazed at you guys. You've all seriously lost your heads over somebody."

A.J.'s laugh filled the warm air. He drove another nail in and looked over at Boston. "That's true enough, wouldn't you say, Charlie?"

Boston shrugged but didn't look up. "Unfortunately." He pulled the trigger and fired off another nail.

"It's a weakness of the male species," Mandy told them matter-of-factly. "You're built to break."

A.J.'s hearty laugh rumbled the framing. He stood. "That's for sure." His finger skimmed the tip of Mandy's nose. "Pretty perceptive, baby doll. Where'd you get all this insight?"

Mandy lifted a shoulder, keeping an occasional glance angled at Boston who stood wiping the saw dust from his hands. His dark eyes locked on the two of them. "Eighteen years of being female will teach you a few things."

"More than a few things," A.J. laughed. "You don't mind that I call you baby doll, do you?" he asked, picking up a nail that had dropped.

"Not at all."

"Let's pack it up so your brother can get out of here." A.J. started over toward the stairs.

"So he and Larry can go hunting?" Mandy joked as

she followed him.

A.J. turned a grin over his shoulder. Mandy's fingers flew to her lips when she figured out the double entendre. Guys have any and all things relating to women on the brain twenty-four-seven, she mused. Or maybe it was just because it was nearing dinner and thoughts slid to hunger.

"You want to go get something to eat?" she asked. A.J. was two steps below her on the rickety stairs. Once he hit the main floor, he extended his hand. "Thanks." She took the last three stairs with his hand steadying her.

When she reached the main floor, A.J. yanked the red bandana from his head and scrubbed his hair. "Can't tonight."

"Another time then." Mandy reached down where she'd left their folded shirts and picked up both A.J.'s and Boston's. She held out A.J.'s "You like Mexican food?"

A.J. took the shirt. "Well enough." He slipped it overhead.

"My friends and I hang at this really fun place on State Street called Bajio."

"I've eaten there." A.J. ran his fingers through his hair.

"Great food and it picks up at night with music. No drinking though." Mandy tapped his shoulder playfully. "And no picking up women. It'd be perfectly safe for you and your tattoo."

A.J. gave a slow blink, the corners of his mouth inching up. Mandy couldn't read the look on his face, and that confused her. He reached out a hand and skimmed it along her cheek. "It's not *my* safety I'm worried about."

Mandy's heart skipped. Her cheek tingled where he'd touched it. She stuffed her hands in her back pockets and glanced around. Boston stood a few feet away, statue-still, a curious gaze pointed right at them.

The air swarmed with feisty currents. Mandy felt caught in the middle of something she wasn't sure of. She looked from Boston to A.J. whose green eyes narrowed; flicking from her to Boston.

"Ah," Mandy began, hoping to lighten the mood. "Bahio'd even be safe for you, Boston." She strolled over, casually swinging her arms. "No chance of tipping you off that pedestal. Promise."

His eyes were still on A.J. The air was still thick. Neither man spoke or moved, and beads of perspiration burst all over Mandy's body. *What the heck was this all about?*

Finally, a lazy grin broke the tight line of A.J.'s lips. "I'll take a rain check on that, baby doll." He started toward the truck. "You can count on it," he tossed over his shoulder.

"Okay," she said. "Great."

Mandy watched him join Marc and Larry at the back of the truck and let out a huff of confusion. "Huh." Then she turned her attention to Boston who looked tight as a piece of sheathing. Cautiously she held out the folded tee shirt. "Your shirt."

He plucked it from her hands. "Thanks."

"So, you want to go grab something to eat?" she asked while he slipped it on. The garment skimmed down the bones and muscles of his chest and back, fluttering into place. "I'm starving. Borders was good today, don't get me wrong, but—"

"I can't," he bit out. "Maybe another time."

"Oh. Well, another night. Sure."

"Yeah."

"Something wrong?"

He let out a snort. "Forget it." And started in the direction of the car. Mandy followed him. Darkness seeped into the air like black ink, shadowing his eyes, the rigid contours of his cheeks and jaw.

"Did I say something?" Heck if she wasn't totally lost. "If you don't like Mexican, just say so," she joked, hoping to lighten the mood.

"Mexican's fine," he said.

"Oh. Good."

His boots dug into the dirt beneath their feet, creating thudding sounds. Her boots tapped lightly next to his. They both reached the truck at the same time and Mandy noticed the fast hush of voices, the way A.J. watched Boston with a keenness that was raw and male. Boston returned the look, jerking his tool belt loose.

Marc's grin was too big and too pleased, and Larry stood there looking like he'd just won a week with the goddess of the month. Mandy unbuckled her belt without saying a word. Something was cooking in the air and it simmered with testosterone.

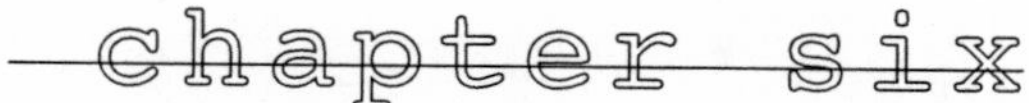

chapter six

Mandy sat on the couch she and Cam usually occupied whenever they had a Borders night. A pile of architectural books lay piled on her lap and at her side but she hadn't opened one. She couldn't stop thinking about the vibe she'd felt between A.J. and Boston.

Next to her, Cam had a pile of romance books equally as impressive as her collection of reading material. His nose was deep into *Three to Tango*. On the cover was a couple dancing.

She wondered if Boston danced.

It was easy to picture him in all black, like the guy on the cover of the book, shirt open, sleek pants like a second skin. To be in his arms, to have him look into her eyes like she was his, moving her across the dance floor to the tango beat... A tingling storm wound through her. But that would never happen. He was stonier than a cornerstone. There was no way to penetrate that level of commitment. And she wasn't sure she wanted to. There was something skanky about setting out to bring somebody down for your own pleasure. She had to resign herself to the fact that the timing was off. She and Boston were never going to be anything but working teammates.

Cam let out a low moan, and Mandy glanced around. "Keep it down," she whispered.

"I love this." Cam shook his head, eyes glued to the open book. "If only this happened in real life, two girls after the same guy. Insane."

"Sometimes it happens."

"Not in my life."

"If you'd spend less time reading about it and get out there, maybe—"

"Nu-uh." Cam's eyes came up to hers. "I'm telling you, this is the plot line of fantasy."

"Guy's fantasy, maybe."

"So if two guys wanted you, you wouldn't be into it?"

"I might be flattered, but I'd probably feel suffocated more than anything else."

"Why suffocated? Enjoy the bounty!" Cam's expression held disbelief. "The love triangle is one of the greatest mathematical configurations God created."

Mandy smiled. "Romance glamorizes everything from kidnappings to love triangles, Cam, you know that. In real life, one person in the triangle hauls off and shoots the competition between the eyes with a sawed-off shotgun."

"Only in extreme cases where psychos are involved." Cam nodded in agreement. "Most of the time it's just people like you and me and the worst thing that happens is an intense fight or, even better, some really hot moments where women's fangs come out." Cam returned to his book.

Mandy frowned. Her mind flashed the scene of earlier, when she'd been in the middle of A.J. and Boston, feeling like a swarm of bees had been let loose.

"So," she began, "How do you know?"

Cam didn't bother looking up, his eyes greedily ate the page in front of him. Mandy extended her leg and tapped her shoe to his, bringing his head up. "What?"

"How do you know?"

"Know what?"

"If there's a triangle."

"For this guy," he pointed to the book, "it's easy. He's the best tango dancer in the world, he can have any woman he wants, and he pretty much dances in and out of the life of every hot babe he can find. Until he meets Sophie. She's different, and doesn't fall for his smooth moves."

Mandy rolled her eyes. "How original."

"Anyway," Cam continued. "He starts to fall for her but then an old dancer from his past comes back into his life and wants him. By this time, Sophie's gotten to see the real him, that he's not just a pro tango dancer. She fights to keep him and Francesca fights to take him away."

"Thank you for explaining the plot line," Mandy said, flatly.

Cam's green eyes sparked. "Classic triangle. Why? You in a triangle?"

Mandy lifted a shoulder, feeling stupid that her thoughts even drifted into something so ridiculous. Cam slapped the book closed and leaned close. "That guy last night, right? Bermuda or Baltimore or whatever his name was."

"*Boston*."

"I knew it." Cam sat back with a satisfied nod.

"How did you know it? I don't even know it for sure."

"It was in his eyes and in the air around us. Man, the minute I walked up he was sizing me up like he wanted to take me out back for a duel."

"K, now you've been reading too many romance books." But a delicious shiver ran down Mandy's spine. "And he was not sizing you up."

"Yes he was."

"Why are you saying this now?"

"What was I gonna say, 'Nice to meet you, but sheathe your sword, dude.'"

Mandy scoffed. "I told you, he got burned bad. He's on sabbatical from women."

"That'll last about one day, trust me."

"You don't know him, he's the iceman. There's no way anybody's gonna melt through him."

Cam's eyes glittered. "You like him, don't you?"

This is where their friendship helped. Mandy could talk to Cam about anything. She tilted her head, an impossibly wide grin on her face gave away her heart. "Yeah, he's interesting."

"So go for it."

"I told you, he's—"

"And I told you that's an overdone cliché."

"But the bet—"

"What bet?"

"Everybody on the team has placed wagers on how long he can stay womanless. We each put twenty-five bucks in the pot and picked a date we think he will…until he…he…"

"Falls?"

"That sounds so sinful, but yeah, basically."

"So how many days did you give him?"

When she only lifted a shoulder, he playfully slugged her. "Okay, don't tell me. But if you want him, take him.

I'm telling you, he wants you too. I can tell. Nothing is cooler to a guy than a woman who knows what she wants and takes it. *Takes*. Man, would I love to be *taken*."

Mandy rolled her eyes. "This stuff you're reading is getting to your head." She took a deep breath. His suggestion that Boston was interested was more thrilling than anything that had happened to her in a while, even surpassing getting her first construction job. The truth surprised her.

"Who else is in the triangle?" Cam picked up his book again, opened it, but looked her in the eye.

"There's another guy that works on the team. He's really nice. Totally fun. Older. Late twenties."

"Perfect."

"What's perfect about it?"

"He's older, more experienced, more *male* if you will. Man," he shut his book, "this is cool. Do you know how lucky you are?"

"I'm not sure this is luck. It's circumstance."

"Freaking fantasy is what it is. Do you like him?"

"I like him, yeah. But not the same way I like Boston."

"But he likes you?"

"I don't know." Mandy chewed her lower lip. "He's always really teasey with me. We have a lot of fun together and he's easy to talk to. But today, he and I were working and I...I..." It was vain to imply such a ridiculous notion, Mandy wasn't sure she could.

"You were working, and..." Cam urged.

"When work was over, I asked A.J. – that's his name – if he wanted to go grab something to eat. He couldn't. Then I asked Boston. He couldn't either. But the two of them stood there like...I don't know, it was just weird."

"Like? Come on, you're killing me here!" Cam tossed aside his book and drove his hands into his hair. "You're living this totally rocking fantasy and you're not basking in it, relishing it, feasting on it."

"Nothing happened," Mandy said. "They just looked at each other like they were—"

"Wait, here, listen." Cam peeled through the book, then held up a finger as he read. "The air sizzled like a million snakes loose on the floor. Octavio—that's the tango-guy's name— stood between Sophie and Francesca, looking from the blazing blonde to the ravishing redhead. Two fires danced in the air, the flames reaching, whipping out in a silent, frenzied fight. One way or the other, Octavio was going to get burned." Cam closed the book, his electric expression on hers. He leaned close, his voice dropped to a whisper. "Was that what it was like?"

Mandy swallowed a lump. "Kinda, yeah."

"Oh, man." Cam fell back into the cushions of the couch, a grin so big on his face it annoyed Mandy.

"Oh, man, what?" she hissed. "It wasn't cool. I felt weird about it."

"Then you're a wuss," Cam shot. "Boston's jealous. P.J., D.C. or whatever his name is, likes you. So use it. Play with it. Go out with P. J. and you'll melt Boston faster than an ice cube on pavement."

"I can't use A.J. That would just be wrong."

"So what? You said he's older, right? He's probably been used and abused before in the name of love. He can take it."

"This isn't love." Mandy wet her lips. A.J. had been burned too and she was sure that flower tattoo wasn't his only scar. She shook her head. "Can't do it."

"Why?"

"Because it's wrong."

"Why? Think about it, Mand." His eyes searched hers. "Maybe, deep down, you like him too."

Mandy bit her lower lip. In her mind, she saw A.J.'s twinkling eyes and lazy smile, and a slow heat started somewhere deep inside she couldn't deny. It wasn't like the heart-stopping, breathless, weak-kneed reaction Boston created. "A.J. sees me like a kid sister."

"That's possible, but it's also possible he looks at you as this fresh, sweet flavor of the month."

Mandy's face twisted. "He'd never think that. He's a gentleman."

Cam's left brow lifted over a wry smile. "Yeah, your typical construction worker."

"That's just it, he's not. Neither is Boston."

"And that's why the three of you are gravitating together. Look, Mand, you can rationalize all you want, but here are the facts: day after day you work together in the smoldering heat. You've got four alpha males and one innocent female. Mix it all together and you might as well be watching a National Geographic special. It's about the animal in all of us, and you're the prize whether you like it or not."

Mandy's heart thrummed out of control. Cam gave her a confident nod then picked up his book.

Knowing was one thing, suspecting was something else altogether. Because Mandy didn't know for sure what was going on between her, Boston and A.J., she wanted to hide. Besides being impossible, the reaction was so lame, she wanted to kick herself.

While the guys got their coffee inside the Haynes main office, she waited out by the truck, a flock of butterflies loose in her stomach. What would work be like today? Without a clue, and no idea how to proceed, she decided professionalism was the only way to handle on-site relationships and that meant being herself: friendly, hard working and focused on the task at hand.

She heard the low rumble of male voices come around the corner of the building but didn't look over from her perch on the back of the truck. A.J.'s husky laugh sent a tremor through her and she almost stole a peek at the lot of them, but stared out at the main highway instead.

"Hey, there she is," A.J.'s tone was friendly, and she couldn't help but turn. They made quite a sight the four of them in their shorts and tee shirts. Builders. Rugged. Male conquerors. A.J. sauntered along with his Styrofoam cup in hand, steam fingering into the morning air. A step behind him was Boston, hands swinging comfortably at his sides. Marc and Larry were together, both laughing, no doubt about last night's conquests. She'd heard Marc stumble into the house after two a.m. last night.

"No coffee this morning?" A.J. stopped close enough that his chest nearly touched her knees. He smiled at her over the rim of his cup.

"No. Not this morning."

Boston caught the distance between her knees and A.J.'s chest, she noticed, and something flashed in his dark eyes.

"Hold this for me, will you, baby doll?" A.J. held out the coffee to Mandy while he hoisted himself up and swung a leg over the back of the truck. Then he held out his hand and she gave him back the cup. "Thanks."

Mandy glanced at Boston, who'd shoved his hands in his front pockets. The corners of his jaw locked tight. "Morning," she said.

"Morning."

"Mand," Marc announced. "You and Charlie ride up front with me."

Mandy's eyes widened. He'd never assigned seats before, what was this all about? Too uncomfortable to ask why or protest, Mandy jumped down, wiped off the seat of her jeans and got in the cab.

She felt trapped by something she couldn't see, yet driven to flee by another unseen source. The truck shifted as the guys loaded in. She sat still, highly aware of Boston when he slid in next to her. His knee brushed hers, skin on denim. She knew his scent now, and it filled her head, misting her mind.

Marc got in and started the engine. He reached over and flicked off the radio then pulled the truck onto the main road. No radio? Marc? Something was wrong.

Mandy took a deep breath. Her gaze was magnetically drawn to Boston's tan thighs precariously close to hers. To his arms, his hands resting on his thighs, his long fingers spread. He had a fresh cut on one finger and a splinter of pain jagged through her looking at the wound, thinking about him hurt in any way.

"Ouch." She reached out and touched the spot. "You should put antibiotic ointment on that and cover it with a Band-Aid." She looked up into his eyes, inches away, those deep brown caverns even more enticing up close.

"It's got one of those liquid, invisible Band-Aids on it."

Mandy swallowed, nodded. "Oh. Does it hurt?"

He seemed pleased and surprised that she asked. "No."

Sweat gathered on the back of her neck. *Why didn't I wear shorts?* It was going to be another killer-hot day and she'd cook in her jeans.

"Stop by the house on the way, will you?" she told Marc, breaking the silence.

"Why?"

"We have the time." She looked at the clock in the car. "There's something I need to do."

"What?"

She cocked her head at him. "*Something*, now do it."

"Why should I? If you forgot *something* that's your problem."

"Fine, then drop me off at home during lunch."

Marc steered with one hand, the other rubbed at his jaw. "Is it—you're not on your—"

"Marc! No." Shock bolted from Mandy's face to her toes and she shrunk in the seat.

"Good. Okay. Cause, that's like the only reason I'd take you home."

"Certainly not out of the kindness of your heart."

"Hey, you're on work time now. Kindness has nothing to do with it."

Mandy shot a glance at Boston. He didn't smile, but silent compassion was on his face.

"So." Marc sat forward, looking at the two of them.

"You two will work together from here on out."

Mandy's brows knit. The confusion on her face had Marc nodding. "That's right. Charlie's been on the team for a while now. He can show you anything I can. He knows what to do."

She scrunched her face at him. *What was he doing? Pushing her at Boston?* "Dad prefers it if apprentices rotate. That way they get exposed to a variety."

"Yeah, I know. But this is my job, and I'm running it my way."

Mandy started to fume. There was only one reason Marc was pushing her at Boston, and that was the bet. Why else would he care? She crossed her arms over her chest. "Boston's a good worker, there's no doubt about that." But she wouldn't dream of compromising his vow to stay as far away from females as possible. "But why not keep to the rotation? You're not trying to compromise Boston's vow, are you?"

"What the crap?" Marc sneered out but avoided her gaze.

Mandy lifted her chin and smiled. Nothing was more satisfying than beating Marc at his own game.

"I'm the boss here, and you'll do what I tell you," Marc shot.

Mandy ticked her finger back and forth under his nose and shook her head. The gesture infuriated Marc. "Let's not lose it here, Marc. It's just a day job."

"Just *your* day job, and you're gonna lose it if you don't—"

"It's okay." Boston's sharp tone cut through their bickering, bringing both Mandy and Marc's attention to him. "Really, it's okay. I don't want you losing your job over this."

"Smart," Marc nodded. "Listen to him, Mand."

Mandy studied the determined lines and angles of Boston's face. "You sure? Because I don't...I wouldn't—"

"You won't."

Mandy's heart plummeted. A slug in the stomach would have hurt less. She turned her gaze out to the front window at the long, empty road ahead.

If framing was anything, it was repetitive—day after day of measuring, sawing, fitting, nailing. Mandy and Boston continued where Boston had left off. Across the room, A.J. worked solo, whistling every now and then. Mandy didn't feel like talking, so she listened to another one of Larry's raunchy CDs and guy talk, holding the other end of the measuring tape when Boston measured. Carrying four-by-sixes, holding beams in place.

"You should have seen this animal last night," Marc called from across the second floor where he and Larry worked. "Not just one, but three women." Marc shook his head and bent over to gather a stack of wood fittings.

"How'd you manage that?" A.J.'s eyes twinkled with amusement.

Larry stopped hammering, turned with a grin and lifted his shoulders.

"First, there was this gorgeous blonde, a Pamela Anderson look alike. She was all over him. What was her name, dude?"

Larry lifted a shoulder. "Heck if I know."

"Another dollar in the pot." Marc shook his head. "Then this cute little cheerleader type did cartwheels for him, right there at the bar. Bet you don't remember her name, either."

"Nope."

"Lastly, this brunette comes along, hair down to her waist, legs up to here." He held his hand to the middle of his chest.

"She was mighty fine," Larry agreed. "Samantha."

All noise came to an abrupt stop, along with any movement. Only the rock music blared on from the boombox. Larry's light eyes widened. "What?"

"You remembered her name." Shock lined Marc's tone.

Larry scratched his head and shrugged. "Guess so."

A.J. resumed hammering. Mandy's eyes met Boston's. He seemed unimpressed by Larry's news and got back to work.

"I couldn't even get one babe to let me buy her a drink and this guy was surrounded like Justin Timberlake." Marc grunted, dropping the wood closer to the window he was framing.

"That brunette liked you," Larry pointed out. "You two looked pretty cozy when you were dancing."

"Yeah but it ended there."

Mandy rolled her eyes. Did everything have to be about hooking up? Was every male that desperate to do the deed? She stole a look at Boston's face, hard lined and focused on what he was doing. If all males were like Larry and Marc, it really would be a feat of willpower for him to stay celibate.

And what about A.J.? His participation in these rank conversations was usually minimal. Something about him set him apart, but Mandy wasn't sure what it was other than age and maturity. Maybe he had a will of stone like Boston. Or maybe he was above all this stuff.

"You're kinda quiet today." A.J. held a post in

one hand, hammer poised in the other. His green eyes flickered over her with the warmth of a blanket. "You okay, baby doll?"

Mandy held a four-by-six in place for Boston who was digging in his tool belt for nails. "I'm fine, thanks, A.J." She liked that he was astute enough to notice, and mature enough to say something.

A.J. drove in a nail. "You know, construction sites are like psychiatrists offices, only better."

Mandy enjoyed her first laugh of the day. "Oh? How's that?"

"You can talk all you want to a listening ear." A.J. readied another nail, holding it in place. "And pound something at the same time."

"Sounds like a deal."

"Does wonders for anger management." A.J. crossed the floor with a glittering grin, reached over and picked up another piece of wood. "And you can't beat the price."

"I imagine it would." Mandy moved with Boston to where a window would be framed in next. Boston dug out the measuring tape, pulled the end out and held it out to her. Their eyes met for half a second.

"Thanks," he said.

"You're welcome." She stood still while he dragged the tape back twelve feet, plucked a marking pencil out of his tool belt, drew a slash on the wood, then stuck the pencil between his teeth.

As the sun snuck upward and heat intensified, sweat drooled down her legs, dripped between her breasts, drizzled down her spine. When Boston came toward her for the loose end of the measuring tape, her heart banged against her ribs.

He snapped the tape back into place and measured the height of the window. With both hands, Mandy lifted her hair off her neck and let out a sigh. Eyes closed, she took in a deep breath of stifling air. "It's gotta be over a hundred today," she murmured.

"Around one-oh-five I bet," A.J. piped.

She kept her eyes closed, feeling the beads of sweat stream every inch of her skin. She couldn't wait until lunch, to get out of these hot jeans and get into something cooler. She'd shied away from shorts because of the hazards of the job, but hazard or not, she'd give them a try. When she opened her eyes, the room wobbled, then blurred and she blinked, wiping the sweat from her face. She blinked again. Sit. She needed to sit down.

Her knees buckled and she plunked to the sub floor. Everything spun. The wood vibrated beneath her and soon both A.J. and Boston were squatted down in front of her. A.J. had his hands on her shoulders.

"You okay?" He was looking her right in the eye. She tried to focus on him and blinked hard again.

"Yeah, yeah. I'm fine. Just a little light headed there for a minute."

"Go get her some water," A.J. tossed to Boston. Boston was gone in another heavy blink.

Mandy knew she'd be history if Marc saw her like this, so she struggled to her feet. A.J.'s sturdy hands helped lift her and stayed on her shoulders until she was steady. Then his strong grip slid to her cheeks. He cupped her face and brought her gaze to his. "When was the last time you drank anything?"

Mandy shrugged. She still felt uneasy, her legs like strings. "I don't know. Maybe…" She hadn't had anything since breakfast, she remembered now, but wouldn't tell him that.

"You need to drink every hour at least."

She nodded. The palms of his hands stayed locked on her cheeks.

Boston bounded back with the water and held it out for her. A.J. grabbed it, ripped off the lid and gave it to her. "Come on, drink. Now."

Mandy wrapped shaking fingers around the bottle, pressed it to her mouth and drank. The icy cold was so blissful; she closed her eyes as the cold liquid went down.

"What the hell were you doing?" A.J.'s hard tone shocked her eyes back open. He was glaring at Boston. "You're supposed to make sure she gets a water break every hour."

Boston's body tensed. He set his hands on his work belt. The flash in his eyes told Mandy he wasn't happy about being accused. "I'm sorry."

"It's not his fault," Mandy said. "I'm my own responsibility."

"No, baby doll. That's why there's an apprentice and a trained team member assigned to them." He slid his glare back to Boston. "She's your responsibility."

Boston dipped his head. His fingers dug into the tool belt at his waist. Mandy looked from one man to the other. "I can take care of myself. Look, I got dehydrated. That's nobody's fault but my own. It was stupid, but it wasn't his fault."

"Hey," Marc's voice sliced through the tension. They all looked at him. "Something wrong?"

"We're good, boss," A.J. said with a wave. A.J.'s gaze wasn't angry anymore. In spite of the pressure in the air, Mandy shivered when his green eyes shifted to hers and something cold there trickled through her. Confused, she waited for him to say something, but he didn't, he just held her under a frosty stare.

"I'm sorry," she repeated. "I'm willing to take responsibility for the oversight."

A.J. stepped back, signaling he was going back to work. "Just take care of yourself. We're here to work, not monitor each other's health." He turned and headed back to his work area.

Mandy took a deep breath. Stepping on the toes of fellow workers was juvenile. Done intentionally or accidentally, it didn't shine a favorable light on the employee doing the stepping.

Boston's perturbed expression wasn't helping matters, either. "I really am sorry," she said to him. He turned and returned to work. Mandy stood in the middle of the empty room, Boston to her left, A.J. at her right. This wasn't as much a triangle, she thought looking from one simmering man to the other, as it was a teeter-totter.

Mandy doubted the guys would miss her over lunch. Talk had been minimal on the side of the house where she, A.J. and Boston worked after the dehydration debacle. Marc dropped her off at home without giving her too much trouble, only telling her that she needed to be ready for pick up right at one o'clock. Then the guys took off to eat.

With a pleasurable sigh she peeled off her sweaty jeans and her whole body breathed in the air conditioned air inside the house. *Much better*. Her red *Homes by Haynes* shirt was too wet to wear again so she found a white wife-beater and pulled it overhead. *That ought to keep me cool enough*. And it'd keep her tan growing slow but sure.

Better idea, she thought, reaching for her baby blue bathing suit. Now she'd tan without a lot of lines.

She pulled on the sleek one piece, followed that with matching boy shorts then tied her blonde waves up in a pony tail. She turned in the full-length mirror. *Yup, no chance for tan lines now*. She frowned at her boots and scrunched socks. Boots were mandatory on site, so she couldn't very well wear flip flops. She'd have lines around her ankles. *Dang*. A small price to pay to max out the rest of her tan while she worked.

At one o'clock Marc didn't honk – he blasted the horn. Mandy hadn't had time to eat, so she grabbed a banana and slipped on her sunglasses on her way out the door.

The truck idled in the driveway like a growling beast. Boston stood at the passenger side with the door open and Mandy jogged over. From the bed of the truck, A.J. leaned over the side, a big smile on his face. Larry, who was sitting in the back with him, did a double take and stood up.

Mandy shot them all a grin. "Hey."

"What are you doing?" Marc demanded.

"You want me drive over separately?"

"I'm not talking about the drive to the site," Marc ground out. "What are you wearing?"

Mandy looked down at herself. "I was too hot, and I want to get some color." She climbed into the cab.

"In that?" Marc's voice cranked up a notch.

"Why not?" Mandy asked. Marc stumbled over words. Nothing coherent came out. "You guys wear the equivalent of bathing suits. This will work double duty for me. Come on, let's go."

Marc hung in the open door on the driver's side and looked her up and down. He shook his head. Mandy wondered why Boston hadn't gotten in the car. He stood tentatively at the door. She patted the empty seat beside her. "Come on."

He climbed in. Mandy reached over and turned on the radio. She didn't like any of Marc's preset stations and pressed the scan button.

"Just find something," Marc growled when he finally climbed in.

"I'm trying. You guys force me to listen to raunch on site. I get to pick something decent when we drive." She stopped on a retro eighties station.

"Tomorrow you're not wearing that," Marc told her.

Mandy bristled. "I'll wear what I want."

"Not when it's indecent," Marc snapped. He kept glaring at Boston and Mandy frowned.

"It's a bathing suit and don't be a hypocrite. You pick up women who wear a lot less."

"They're not my sister!"

"Thankfully," she shot back. "I just want to stay cool and get a tan. It's over a hundred degrees outside, Marc. What's fair is fair, right Boston?"

Boston's jaw was in a knot. His hands, resting on his thighs, were tense, his fingers digging. He only glanced at her.

"You're siding with him?" she nearly shrieked. "Unbelievable." She folded her arms.

"There's a difference," Marc snapped.

"What? Tell me? I guarantee if we measured bare skin inch for inch, you guys would have more naked flesh than me. Guarantee it."

"It's the flesh that's bare that's the problem, Mand." His eyes were hard flicking over her. "You've got...got... stuff."

Mandy laughed. "You can hanker after it but you can't bring yourself to use the correct terms?"

"Hey, when I hanker, I hanker after women I don't know."

"And that's a healthy male thing to do," Mandy argued back. "So what are you worried about?"

"You prancing around the site."

"Prancing?" Her laugh was sharp. "I'm working, just like you guys."

Marc rubbed his jaw. "You don't get it."

"What I get is that you run your site with a double standard. From day one you haven't wanted me to work with you, and so you're taking it out on me every way you can. It's unfair and unprofessional."

"That is not true. Okay, part of it might be. But that's not what I'm talking about right now."

They were almost at the site, and Mandy couldn't wait to get out of the close confines of the car. It was embarrassing that they were having this dispute in front of Boston and she looked at him. "I'm sorry about this," she said.

He cleared his throat. "I agree with him."

Mandy's mouth opened but nothing came out—for a second. "You agree?"

He looked like he'd swallowed a thousand crickets. "It's..." His gaze skimmed her and Mandy felt like he'd brushed fire over her skin. Then he looked at Marc.

"Forget it," he said.

Mandy thought she knew guys pretty well, but the last few days had shown her just how much she still had to learn about the simple complexities of the male species.

At the site, Marc jerked the truck to a stop. Boston got out and immediately went around to the back of the truck to belt up. Marc leaned close enough to Mandy to startle her. "You don't get it, do you?" he whispered.

"Back to this again?" she hissed. Out the rear window of the cab, she saw the guys gathered around the storage box.

"You're going to distract them dressed like that."

She only paused a second, stunned. "I work here. They don't see me like girl, they see me as a fellow worker, something you might try."

"Right. They don't see you as a girl. That bathing suit screams woman."

Mandy flushed from head to toe. At last her brother saw her for what she had struggled for so long to be. It wasn't just the change in her attire that had done it, either. It came from being seen that way in the eyes of his peers. If she gloated, he'd kill her, so she merely lifted her chin and kept her grin under control. "I'll take that as a compliment, Marcus." Then she got out and shut the door.

There was power in her stride now, awareness that the playing field was not just even, but maybe even tilted in her favor. The guys' heads jerked up and all eyes were on her. She smiled when they parted for her. "Hey."

"You want your belt, baby doll?" A.J.'s grin seemed permanent. He already had the belt in his hands, and held it out to her.

"Thanks, A.J." She slipped it around her waist. After securing the buckle, she looked up. The guys stood immobile, attention locked on what she was doing.

Marc was busy getting his own tool belt on but he hadn't missed the stupor the guys were in. He cleared his throat. Larry let out a whistle before heading into the house. A deep flush covered Boston, who dipped his head before taking off for the second floor.

"You mean to drive us all crazy today?" A.J.'s grin deepened. The look in his eyes was something Mandy had never seen in the eyes of any of the guys she'd spent time with: sharp, powerful, and almost peeled her bare. As if he knew exactly how he was making her feel.

"I just want to stay cool and get a tan…like you guys."

A.J. wrapped his red bandana around his head, his gaze lingering over her so calculatedly, she almost wanted to cover herself. Almost. Another part of her enjoyed the way he took her in, as if he was sweeping her inside of himself with just a look.

He finished knotting the bandana and started toward the house, backwards. "Don't forget the sunscreen. Wouldn't want you to get burned."

Marc stomped over, kicking dust up around them.

"Marc, chill." Mandy adjusted the heavy belt around her waist so it lay flush with the waist of her bathing suit and shorts. "He's not interested in me that way." She watched his face for a reaction, curious if he'd seen anything, sensed what she had sensed about A.J. and Boston. Only anger bubbled in his expression, and she was relieved. There was no triangle. The idea was nothing more than Cam's desperate male imagination, and he'd infected her with it.

"You've got a lot to learn." Marc spit on the ground, his gaze narrow.

"And I intend to." Mandy walked with him into the house. "I'm watching, Marc. And I'm picking everything up. I can do this."

He stopped, and leveled her with a look that made her feel like a girl again. "You still think this is about work?" He shook his head and went upstairs.

chapter eight

Mandy couldn't move, cut down by Marc's remark. She prided herself on being intuitive. She'd always been able to read Marc like a blueprint; he was about as predictable as a tract house.

So why did she have this cramp of uncertainty in her stomach?

She almost snatched a company tee shirt out of the back of the truck but decided against it. That wouldn't prove anything. Just seconds ago she'd been sure the playing field was tilted in her favor. After Marc's comment, nothing was even, everything was distorted.

She couldn't let it stop her from doing her best work and moving ahead with goals. Being accepted as one of the crew in every sense of the word was what her apprenticeship was about.

She took the stairs up, her chin held high, and crossed directly to Boston who had already started on the next section of interior wall. A.J. winked at her from across the room. A fast blush covered her skin but she made sure her hips moved with just enough sway to signal that she wasn't backing down about what she'd chosen to wear or more importantly, that she was there to work.

Larry's music screamed. The whole structure rocked and shimmied like a pool hall at midnight. For a guy who didn't like to dance, she questioned Larry's choice of music. Whatever was playing sounded like it was piped right from the nearest club.

Protocol demanded that she ask Boston for an assignment. He had his back to her, pounding nails in. His tool belt hung askew on his narrow hips and the sight was cute. Mandy smiled. "Where do you want me?" she asked.

He pounded one of two nails he held between his fingers into the piece he was securing and jerked his head right, indicating a pile of wood. "Cut me some base pieces for this wall."

She nodded. The sun bit mercilessly into her skin, but it felt good. At least she wasn't baking in jeans. Her deep breath took in the scent of sunscreen she'd slathered on, as well as the elixir of wood, and gave her a natural high. Dutifully, she followed Boston's directions and over the next few hours the final wall along the west side of the house slowly erected.

Boston levered the last, long piece into place and Mandy stepped close, reached out and centered it, holding it in place for him. Sweat dripped in long streams down his spine. The tips of his dark hair clung in wet waves around his face. His dark eyes met hers and Mandy's heart fluttered.

"You should take a water break," he said, fingers dipping into the nail pocket on his belt.

Real caring was behind the suggestion, and Mandy appreciated that. "Just as soon as we're done."

He smiled a little, planted the nail and hammered. Then he dropped down. Up until that moment, her choice of attire hadn't bothered her, but the minute Boston was down at her knees and her fantasy kicked in, every cell in her body ripped open, vulnerable and exposed. Clothes really did help protect you, she thought, noticing the brown color of his crown. Maybe males grew up without that added layer of security because they spent more time with their skin exposed than females. All she knew was that what had seemed practical, now felt dreadfully uncomfortable. She tried to cover herself with her free hand but wasn't able to.

Finally, Boston drove in the last nail. He tested the post with a firm shake, then stood, his gaze following the lines of her body from her calves to her thighs past her tool belt with a fast leap to her face. Her breath stalled in her chest. Her pulse thundered.

"You look like you're getting burned," he said.

Mandy took a deep breath. "Oh?"

He scratched the back of his head, nodded, and pointed to a couple of spots on her shoulders. Hesitantly, he nodded at one on her chest. She looked down. Sure enough her chest was scarlet.

"You have any sunscreen?" he asked.

"In my haste to cool off, I forgot to bring some. But I did put some on earlier."

"Hmm."

It was cute the way his lips twisted, the way he kept scratching his head like he wasn't sure what to do.

"Hey, A.J." She started over to him. "Do you have any sunscreen?"

"Yeah, just a sec." A.J. finished, slipped his hammer into his tool belt and met her halfway. His eyes made a quick scan of her. "You're red, baby doll." He reached behind and pulled out a small tube of sunscreen then handed it to her.

"Thanks." Mandy started the process of rubbing the white cream into her shoulders and arms.

"You're skin's fair," A.J. commented.

"A curse."

"What curse?" A.J. asked. "It's like porcelain. Be glad. Some men like that."

Mandy flushed but met his gaze. "Oh, yeah? I think you're just saying that so I don't feel like an albino next to you. Look." She held her arm up against his. His skin was rough and dark compared to her pale excuse for a tan. "Look at that," she said.

"Like I said," his voice scraped and she looked at him. Controlled intensity was in his eyes again, shooting sparks off inside of her. "The contrast is what's beautiful."

Mandy swallowed a thick knot. Before she knew it, A.J.'s fingers slipped the tube from her hand, squeezed some lotion into his palms and then he was behind her, rubbing and spreading the cool cream into the tender skin across her back. She winced.

"You're pretty red here," his voice was low and husky, his touch gentle. Mandy'd never had a massage before, but knew in that instance, it would be intoxicating. His hands slid down her back, along her sides and Mandy broke out in laughter when his fingers skimmed side zones particularly ticklish.

"Thanks, A.J." She turned and took a step back, along with a much needed breath.

"No problem." A.J. rubbed his hands together. Behind him stood Boston, arms crossed over his chest, dark eyes razor sharp and aimed right at the two of them.

Boston turned and headed downstairs. Mandy bit her lower lip. This whole situation was too sticky for her liking. She felt A.J. come up behind her. The scent of his sweat mixed with the fragrance in the sunscreen now on her skin.

"You had anything to drink?" he asked.

"I was just going down to get something." She turned. He was still rubbing leftover cream into his hands. His grin had faded into something subtle, ponderous.

He kept glancing toward the stairs where Boston had just disappeared. At the same time, he held her there with a gaze that pricked Mandy's curiosity, like an enticingly wrapped present that was forbidden, but she was still tempted to open. She understood that opening it might be dangerous.

She backed toward the stairs. "You want anything to drink?"

"Sure. Yeah. I'll take a water."

Sweat cooled as she took the stairs down into the shade on the first floor. Boston was already by the cooler, bent over, rifling through it. He didn't look at her, even when she stopped next to him. After he'd grabbed a bottle, she quickly grabbed two and opened one.

He was in the middle of a long chug, so she took the moment to quench her thirst as well. He emptied the whole bottle, wiped his mouth and finally looked at her.

Her stomach did a somersault. "Hey," she said.

"Hey."

"You okay?" She tightened the lid on her bottle.

"Yeah." He turned, tossed the empty bottle into a corner and started back upstairs. Mandy followed, wanting more than anything to restore the light, fun atmosphere that had been in the air when she'd first come on the job.

Boston went right back to work; A.J. stopped and came over, his lazy grin back in place. "Thanks." He took the water bottle, untwisted the lid. "We're making progress," he said with a look around. "Right on schedule. That ought to make Marc happy."

Mandy nodded. "It's Friday, that'll make Marc happy enough."

"True." A.J. chuckled, took a long drink. "You going to that Mexican place you were telling me about this weekend?"

"I haven't made plans yet."

"I don't get it," A.J. studied her. "A cutie like you shouldn't have a minute to spare."

"Well I don't. I mean, I work all day, and you know how time consuming that can be. And then I—"

"I'm not talking about that." He shook his head on a low laugh. "I'm talking about the men in your life. They should be camped out on your doorstep." Mandy dipped her head. "That's the problem with younger guys," A.J. went on. "They haven't been out there long enough to recognize a pearl when they see it."

Words scrambled then evaporated from Mandy's mind. She was flattered and embarrassed at the same time, to have such an appraisal. "Thank you, but I'm not sure I'm much of a pearl."

A.J. reached out and touched the tip of her chin, then took another drink, his green eyes staying with hers. "Even you don't see it. But then that's part of what makes you special."

"Thanks, A.J. Your sisters taught you well, didn't they?"

He laughed, the water bottle poised at his lips. "I

guess they had something to do with it. School of hard knocks is where most of us learn. I'm no different."

"The one university we all have to attend," Mandy joked.

"Mandy."

Boston's sharp call had Mandy whipping around. He stood waiting alongside the spot where the inside wall they were set to erect was set to go up. He had his arms across his chest and a scowl on his face.

"Can we get back to work now?"

"Oh. Um, sure." Mandy started over.

"Thanks for the water, baby doll." A.J. lifted the now-empty bottle at her and she smiled.

"No problem." She swung her arms, turned and bumped into Boston. His brown eyes were black, and not amused. They slid from her, over her shoulder to A.J. and held. Mandy didn't dare turn around and see how A.J. took the condemning look.

"I'm all yours," she said, then cringed.

Boston started in on the wall without a word, and she followed suit, measuring, cutting then fitting wood in place. Through the framed rooms on the second floor, Mandy saw that Marc and Larry were making progress on the master bedroom area.

"This is nice floor plan," Mandy commented, thinking about the layout. Boston nodded. "Small but well laid out." She wondered where he lived, was it a house or an apartment. Did he have roommates or did he live on his own.

"You live in a house or an apartment?" she asked.

"Apartment."

"Alone?" When he hesitated, she thought she'd

asked too much of a man bent on keeping personal details at arms length. Maybe he'd lived there with the woman who'd burned and dumped him.

"It's a fourplex I own. I live in one—alone—and rent out the others."

"Smart." Mandy was impressed. She knew enough about real estate, building and investing from her dad to know a move like that meant money in the bank in the long run. "You learn that from Napoleon Hill?"

He shot her a smile, and all of the crimped worry she'd held onto smoothed out. "Not him, another investment guy."

"That's cool that you study investing."

He handed her the dummy end of the measuring tape and stepped backwards. "I don't want to build houses all my life."

"What do you want to do?"

The tape was stretched between them and neither moved for a moment, eyes locked on the other. Boston took in a deep breath. "I'm not sure yet."

"That's cool. You're young still."

Something dark glinted in his eyes and he tugged the tape to the wall and held it firm, measuring. "Compared to what?"

Mandy held her end in place while he marked the measurements with his pencil. "Compared to whatever. You don't have to be on course yet, is all I'm saying."

"You're on course," he said, coming toward her, the tape between them shrinking, drawing them together. He stopped. The toes of his boots touched hers. "You want to build houses."

All she could do was nod, swamped with his aura,

feisty, challenging, tempting. "You know what you want," he nearly whispered. "And you know what you're doing."

Mandy swallowed. She was pretty sure he wasn't talking about her career choice anymore.

He hooked the measuring tape to his belt but his gaze never left hers, as if he was trying to read her, to measure the truth. Mandy hated the apprehensiveness she saw behind his eyes, that need to protect a vulnerable heart. She felt the urge to reach out and comfort him, but didn't. She wouldn't be the one to bring him down. The heat, the close proximity of the work, the long days building something together, all of it was tightening their bond, constructing a relationship of friendship she would not jeopardize. She might never have him any other way, but they worked together, and that was better than nothing at all.

He lowered his gaze to the dusty sub floor and his dark lashes fluttered against his cheeks. Mandy bit her lip, watching him struggle with what to trust, what to believe. More than wanting him at that moment, she understood what her heart really needed to do. She didn't want him to be hurt again—by anyone—not even her. If he thought she wasn't interested, he'd step back, stay in the safe zone and his heart could get stronger before he took another chance.

She crossed the room, picked up an armful of cut two-by-fours and brought them to where they would begin the next section of inner wall for one of the bedrooms. It only took him a few minutes before he joined her, and they were back at work as a team.

• • • • •

The sun was gone, but its deep fiery rays clung to the sky, oozing, melting away like paint dripping down a wall. Marc carried the cooler to the truck, the ice inside sloshing with each of his steps. He opened it, dumped the remaining water bottles out and poured the residual water out before hefting the cooler up and plopping it in the back of the truck where A.J., Mandy and Boston stood stowing their tool belts.

"Man, it was a bugger today." Marc swiped his hand over his face.

Larry had already taken off his tool belt and stood a few feet away emptying the rest of his water bottle over his head. "At least, dude."

Having packed her tool belt safely away, Mandy decided Larry's idea was the perfect way to end the day and she grabbed a bottle then moved away from the back of the truck and the tool chest. She twisted off the lid and held it up over her head. The icy streams brought a high-pitched squeal from her throat, and the cold water nearly sizzled on contact with her skin.

"Aah, this feels great," she murmured, eyes closed as the cool liquid drenched her. She swiped her arm across her eyes feeling more refreshed, and opened her eyes just in time to catch A.J., Larry and Boston watching. Boston quickly looked away, but A.J.'s lips lifted in a grin.

"What're you doing?" Marc was by her side, scowling. "Wasting water like that."

"Larry's doing it," Mandy protested, pointing at Larry who instantly ditched his water bottle.

Marc reached into the back of the truck, snagged a tee shirt and tossed it in her face. "Yeah, well, Larry's not built like you. Put this on."

Mandy crushed the tee shirt in two tight fists. She'd had plenty of fights with Marc over the years, and knew his anger patterns as well as she knew how to start a fire from scratch. But the blaze covering his face was already scorching. In two giant steps he had her by the arm and was hauling her to the cab of the truck.

"Hey!" She finally ripped her elbow free when they were at the door.

"Get in the truck," he snapped, opening the door.

"It's two hundred degrees in there!" She glanced around, saw that the guy's heads' were averted and she lowered her voice. "You're acting like a retard here."

"Well it's five hundred degrees out here with you in your wet bathing suit." He leaned close, sending her back against the hot steel of the car. She screeched. Concern flashed over his face and he turned her around for a look at her back. "Jeeze. You okay?"

She batted away his hands. "I'm fine. *Fine*. What's with you?"

"I just...I don't like those guys looking at you."

"Nobody was looking, Marc." She yanked the tee shirt over her head.

"Guys always look," he said, keeping his voice between them. "Put a beautiful woman in front of their faces and they start drooling. It's automatic, Mand. Like pressing a button and turning on the coffee maker."

He looked so worried, Mandy almost laughed, but she couldn't. He'd shove her in the car. He'd called her beautiful. He'd never done that before. She reached out and patted his face. "Thanks, but I can take care of myself."

A smile creased his lips. "I know. You're not a kid anymore. I'm just telling you, be careful."

"Have I ever been anything else?" She tilted her head. The guys were done drinking water and she could tell by the way Larry shifted his feet and loudly sighed, they were anxious to be on their way.

"You're in a whole new world here, Mand." Marc stepped back, dug in his pocket and got out his keys.

"Sounds like a song I once heard," she teased, starting toward the truck bed.

"But this isn't Disneyland," Marc called to her. She pulled herself up and into the back hoping he'd get the message that she was going to ride there and not in the cab. He got into the cab without saying anything more. Mandy sat down on the cool bed liner and stretched out, resting her head against the wheel indentation. A bridge had just been crossed, and it felt good to be on the other side. She and Marc had been at odds, fighting their way across the wobbly conduit for some time now. She breathed in a contented breath.

The truck shimmied as the rest of the guys took their places, and the motion rocked her into a peaceful relaxed state that could carry her into sleep if she let it. The diesel engine roared, then growled low and steady when the truck started off.

The feeling that she was being watched had her opening her eyes and looking into A.J.'s cool, green gaze. He sat across the truck bed, arms stretched out, legs extended, his legs nearly side-to-side with hers. He'd taken off his red bandana, and now his caramel-colored hair was mussed from the wind. The corners of his mouth lifted slow and easy.

"Tired?" he asked over the engine's hum

She sat up, blinked, and looked at the backs of Marc, Larry and Boston's heads in the cab. "A little."

"Too tired to hang out?"

She looked at him—at the man across from her. Definitely a man. Older, wiser. His face, his body, every part of him that much more etched by life than any of the boys she'd hung out with. Her decisions had always been driven by curiosity, but this step was in uncharted territory, just like Marc had said. She wasn't in Disneyland.

"With you?"

He gave her a heavy blink. "You okay with that?"

Her throat closed suddenly, so she nodded, then swallowed. "Sure. Of course. It'd be fun."

"Good."

Mandy's insides scrambled and a chill spread under her skin. It wasn't like she was worried. Or afraid. It wasn't about being in danger or anything like that. A.J. was a gentleman, had manners, and knew how to treat a woman; he'd demonstrated that more than once now. Conversation wasn't a problem when you could see where you stood in the safe confines of a framed room. But they'd be alone, not at some loud, crowded bowling alley hanging in a group like she was accustomed to, because that's not what men and women did. You graduated from hanging in groups to going solo, that was the point.

Like going to Italy to study the Parthenon. Alone.

When the truck idled to a stop back at the home office, A.J. got out first and held his hand up for Mandy so she could disembark with finesse. She had to admit she liked the girly treatment after a long day of sweat and raunchy talk. The guys spilled out of the cab just in time to witness the gentlemanly gesture.

Not only was Boston tuned in, but Mandy knew darned well that Marc's brother antenna was cranked up as well.

"So, tonight?" A.J. reached into his pocket for his keys.

Mandy nodded. "Sure."

"Anybody gonna need their belts over the weekend?" Marc asked. Nobody said yes, each gathering their personal possessions and heading to their cars.

Mandy snuck a glance at Boston, curious whether or not he'd reacted one way or the other to A.J.'s invite. His determined, cool façade was perfectly in place, she noticed. She ignored a pinch of disappointment. It was better that way. The very real fact was that he probably didn't care one way or the other, they were just fellow workers. Friends.

"Eight?" A.J. asked. He walked alongside her toward the other *Homes by Haynes* truck she and Marc had driven from home. Mandy appreciated that Marc was taking his time coming over, allowing them some privacy.

"Eight'd be great," she said, then she gave him her address.

A.J. backed to his car, jingling his keys in his hands. "See you then."

Boston slammed the door of his older pickup truck and started the engine. From across the parking lot, Larry shouted to Marc. "Dude, we on for tonight?"

Marc nodded back. "Yeah. Ten?"

"Right on." Larry dipped into his old, beat up red Mustang and tore out of the parking lot.

Mandy climbed into the truck and looked out the window, her lower lip between her teeth. Boston. Well, at least he knew she was desirable, even if he wasn't interested. In high school she might have relished the opportunity to make somebody jealous, but she saw that for the childish, hurtful act that it really was now. An act that wouldn't bring any pleasure to her, bruising an already beaten heart.

Marc got in and shut the door. They drove in silence for a while, not even the radio in the background, and Mandy waited for him to lay into her about A.J. When he didn't, she wondered if she'd made a mistake, accepting A.J.'s invitation, and now Marc was going to sit back and watch her crash and burn enjoying her first tumble in the adult world of men.

"How come you're not ragging on me?" she finally asked, still peering out the window.

"Because you're a big girl, you can make your own decisions."

"Okay, but, what was all this stuff earlier about being

careful."

"It was me giving you my two cents."

"You think A.J.'s okay?" She looked over then, and waited.

His gaze met hers and even in the darkening night, the reassurance she was hoping for was on his face. "Think I'd be sitting here all calm if he wasn't?"

Mandy smiled. "If he was Larry?"

Marc laughed and shook his head. "We wouldn't even be having this conversation if it was Larry."

It was true and Mandy's laugh joined his.

"But I kinda thought you and Boston," Marc said.

"Nah," Mandy lied. Marc had probably placed his money on Boston caving sooner than later, and caving from her advances. If he had, it wouldn't be him taking home the pot if Boston finally broke.

Not that money had anything to do with her decision. She could care less. It was the principle of the idea. Boston's principles specifically, which she wanted to protect and respect.

Marc scrubbed his jaw with his free hand. "I thought the two of you were hitting it off."

"Guess I'm not the only one who has a lot to learn."

"Guess not," he mumbled, pulling into the driveway.

Mandy decided on a lightweight halter sundress with strawberries all over it. Red, jeweled flip flops were the shoe of choice, along with dangling silver earrings. She wore her blond hair down, not bothering to straighten the natural soft waves. The burn she'd acquired that day was pink and tender, and looked as painful as it was becoming. She'd had enough sunburns to know that they intensified as the hours progressed.

At eight, she heard the doorbell, then the low rumble of male voices: Marc and A.J.

Bubbles popped in her stomach as she took the stairs down. She blinked at the man standing in the entry. Dressed in dark slacks and a silky white shirt, hair neatly mussed with gel, A.J. looked like he'd just jumped off the pages of that *Esquire* magazine she'd seen him reading at the bookstore. Whatever cologne he was wearing filled the air with a delicious, spicy scent. His teeth gleamed against his burnished skin.

He turned, his gaze locked on hers. "Hey, there she is. Wow. You look beautiful."

"Thank you." If he'd been any of the guys she'd gone out with in high school, she'd slug him in the arm with a good natured snort. But everything about A.J. lifted her to another place, as if he was on the second floor of the house they were framing, reaching out to pick her up and everything silly and inconsequential would slough away in that one, fast, motion.

"So," Marc nodded, "you guys have fun."

Just like that, A.J.'s hand was there at her waist, gently escorting her to the front door. "See ya," he said.

"Bye, Marc." Mandy took the cue and allowed A.J. to escort her out. The door shut softly behind them. He didn't keep his hand at her back after that, it slid down to his side and they walked together to his car.

"Great house," he said with a look around. "But then I'd expect as much for a builder."

"Dad built it on spec." She was glad to have

something to talk about. He opened the door of his vintage silver Audi, the gesture a first for her. She reminded herself that this was a man that had grown up with sisters.

The car soon filled with everything masculine about him. His smile lit up the dark space. His laugh drowned out the lazy jazz CD taunting the mood in the background, and his cologne snuck on her every breath. Mandy had never had a guy listen so attentively to everything she said, as if she was the most fascinating person on the face of the planet.

Before she knew it, they were downtown at Osaka, a Japanese restaurant. Once again, he got out and opened her door extending his hand so getting out was not only effortless, but looked good.

Again his hand was at her back, and she felt his rough fingertips through the sheer sundress. "You like Japanese food?" he asked. The scent of fried food lingered in the night air. Mandy's stomach responded with a low growl.

Everything was dream like: the kind treatment, the balmy evening, the handsome man. Her mind was bedazzled and she nodded. "Sure."

• • • • •

They ate sushi and tempura. Both drank virgin strawberry daiquiris and talked their way through every subject from the pros of two-by-six versus two-by-four construction, to Mandy's career, to A.J.'s social life.

Mandy stirred what was left of her daiquiri with the tiny paper umbrella that had come perched in the drink.

The evening had done nothing but impress her with the man sitting across from her. She couldn't imagine why he was single.

"So, do you date regularly?" she asked, enjoying that his eyes twinkled with amusement.

"I date enough. Why?"

"You're just so...settled."

"What makes you think I'm settled?"

"Well, you've got a good job. You have a nice car. I'll bet you own a house. And you're twenty....twenty.... how old are you, anyway?"

"Take a guess."

"Don't make me do that, please. I hate offending people when I guess wrong."

"Men don't get offended by that, baby doll. Take a guess."

Mandy's face twisted. "Twenty-eight?"

"Twenty-seven."

"And you're twenty-seven."

"So because I'm old, I should be married?"

"You're not old and you don't have to be married." Heat rushed to Mandy's cheeks. "I'm not the kind to tell other people what they should and shouldn't do."

A.J. leaned forward, his forearms resting on the table, his amused expression electric as his gaze held hers. "That's just one of the things that makes you so irresistible."

A tingle slid down Mandy's spine. She'd never been told she was irresistible before. "Well, I figure everybody's got a right to make their own decisions and live their own life. I mean, I wouldn't want someone telling me what to do. I get plenty of that from Marc."

A.J. reached for his water glass and flicked his wrist so the ice cubes jangled. "He's just looking out for you. My older sisters did the same for me."

"I know he is."

"He'd be crazy not to." He tipped back the last bit of water in his glass then set it down.

"Four sisters did you say?" She leaned on her elbows, her hands clasped at her chin. "No wonder you're so smooth." Mandy cringed when his cocky smile spread. "I don't mean it like…you know, like car salesman smooth. I mean…" She meant experienced. Confident. Sure. "I'm sorry." Heat bled up her cheeks. "That didn't come out right."

His green eyes sparkled in the soft light. "It's okay." He leaned forward and laced his fingers together on the table, holding her gaze tight. "It's refreshing. You say what's on your mind."

He reached out and one of his hands took hers. The touch of his calloused, warm hands sent a shiver through her system. She watched his long, tanned fingers lightly stroke hers.

He took a deep breath and it seemed to Mandy as if he wanted to say something more, but he didn't. He just held her hand, cold and clammy as hers had become, in his warm, rough one.

Mandy swallowed. Never had she been treated with such care and thought. With other boys, she'd felt like a buoy bobbing in the sea, unsure of where the current might take them. In A.J.'s presence she felt safe, like he was in complete control of everything around them in a way that made her feel like she could conquer anything.

"How about a little dancing?" He turned her palm

and traced the lines with one of his fingers, but his gaze stayed on hers. The light touch of his finger caused ripples of sensation to stream from her hand to her pounding heart.

Mandy looked around at the quiet restaurant, almost empty now that it was ten o'clock. An ethnic, twanging melody played from speakers somewhere, but it wasn't the kind of music you could dance to. When she looked at him again, his heavy blink and slow smile reached inside of her like a leisurely caress. "Not here," he said. "Somewhere else."

Mandy took a deep breath. "Okay."

She'd never heard of the place before. It wasn't a club in the sense of an over-eighteen-drinking establishment. It was the Country Club, and on Friday nights a four piece jazz band played in one of the halls.

The room wasn't packed, but Mandy was surprised at the crowd: a mix from teenagers to elderly folks listened to the rowdy, swing beat the band was playing. A.J. seemed to know a few of the faces in the crowd. He slipped his hand around hers and led her through the jumble of couples, right to the middle of the floor.

"You like to dance, don't you?" he asked over the brass.

"I like to but I'm not much of a dancer." Mandy glanced around. Polished dancers seemed to surround them, lifting, twirling, dipping and lunging like they'd just stepped into the middle of a dance show.

A.J. wasn't bad either. Not showy by any stretch,

but he knew how to keep the beat and move himself without looking clumsy. *That's more than I can do*, Mandy thought, unable to stop smiling. It still amazed and thrilled her that he'd actually been paying attention to what she'd said on the job and thought about it enough to bring her to a place where they could dance.

The song ended and everyone on the floor broke out into applause. A leisurely, sumptuous sax played next, and Mandy knew a slow dance was on the agenda. A.J. didn't even let the first few bars of the song go by, he slipped his arms around her, closing the gap between them, and she was next to him from chest to knees. Muscles and male all the way down.

She kept her gaze on the band, feeling his locked on her. Out the corner of her eye, she saw his lips curve into a smile. "You all right baby doll?"

It would have been rude not to meet his gaze then, so she did, ignoring that she'd started to sweat, that her heart was skipping in her chest and she was shaking. "I'm great. This has been great, A.J. Really."

"It has been," he agreed. "You're a good dancer."

Mandy laughed. "There's nothing to bear hugging." Still, she couldn't deny that he held her close, tight, with a poise she'd never felt in the arms of another guy before. In his arms she didn't feel awkward or gangly but protected and...wanted. She wondered how often he'd danced this way.

"How did you find this place? I'd never pegged you for a country club kind of guy," she said, looking at the crystal chandeliers, the mirrored walls, and the blissful faces of the conservative patrons in the room.

"My family has a membership here."

"Oh." She thought that you had to be rich or have an old, established family name to be a member of a club. *He must come from money.* "So you *are* a country club guy."

"You mean old and stiff?"

"Well, kind of, yeah. But you're not snobby at all."

"Thank you."

"Nice clothes, sleek car..." Mandy leaned back in his arms, studying him with a smile. "What do you want to do for a real job?"

His hands tightened briefly around hers but his lazy smile remained. He chuckled. "You don't consider framing a real job?"

"For—" Mandy stopped herself from saying 'guys who couldn't finish an education.' "Did you go to college?"

"Yeah, I went. Got my degree." The slightest thread of defensiveness was in his voice. "Then I decided I didn't want to be an accountant stuck behind a desk all day. I'd rather work with my hands, feel the sun on my face, and be able to dine at fine restaurants like *Hooters* for lunch."

Mandy laughed. At least he had a sense of humor about his future. Still, that he was settled with such a lackluster future wedged under her skin like a sliver. Maybe money came easily for him, easy enough that his motivation was driven by necessity rather than ambition. For now, she'd enjoy his company, soak in the music, the moment, and bask in the movement of his body next to hers.

He continued moving them in a slow lull, like a ship cradled on ocean waves. He adjusted his grip around her and suddenly she was even closer. His green eyes were dark and intensely focused on her mouth. His fingers spread on her bare back, lighting little sparks under her skin. Lightly, gently, his caress moved along her ribs, one of his fingers traced a line of heat down her spine, sending her body into a visible shudder.

"You cold?" he asked.

Her eyes widened. "N-no." Sweat sprung from every pore in fact. She hoped she wasn't shiny, that he couldn't see it. "It's hot. I'm hot. Must be the sunburn. Are you hot?"

His lip lifted on one side. "It's warm in here, yeah."

"Whoo." She slid one hand from his neck and fanned herself, glancing around. "Do you think the air is on?"

He chuckled, low and soft near her ear. "You're trembling."

Mandy's heart nearly jumped from her chest. He could feel that? Fear, fascination, curiosity and something she couldn't identify swam inside her in a turbulence gaining momentum. She felt like she might burst open, right there on the dance floor if she didn't sit down somewhere fast.

"Relax." His voice was lower than the trombone and buzzed next to her ear.

Her heart sped. Her knees weakened.

"Excuse me." She broke free of him, and wound through the other dancers in search of a chair.

Finding one, she nearly collapsed into it. Her skin felt like it was on fire, and that fire was consuming her from the outside in, threatening to converge on her turbulent feelings. Mandy couldn't bear to look at him as he strode quickly to her, concern on his face; she was too embarrassed that she'd ditched him like some junior high nerd at her first dance.

He sat down next to her, his right hand gently on her arm. "You all right?"

Mandy nodded. *How mortifying*. "I'm sorry."

"It's okay. Probably got too much sun today." He pressed the back of his hand first to her forehead, then to her left cheek. "Want to call it a night?"

As if a load of lumber had just been lifted from her body, she felt instant relief and wondered why, when she'd enjoyed herself so much. He still had his hand on her arm, his warmth and hers creating a fusion she couldn't differentiate.

"Maybe I'd better."

She was at a loss for words, humiliated that she'd behaved like a juvenile, and didn't say anything as he walked her to his car. He'd felt her trembling. She closed her eyes and kept her face toward the window. He started the engine.

"Hey." His hand covered hers, resting on her lap. "Baby doll?"

Time to redeem yourself, she thought, opening her eyes and facing him. "This really was fun tonight. I really am sorry I...I..." *panicked*, she thought now, like a girl on her first date. *What a dork*.

He squeezed her hand then returned both palms to the steering wheel. "We had a good time, that's what this was about."

She nodded, that same relief flowing over her she'd felt after she'd left the dance floor. They talked about their favorite types of music the rest of the drive, and

A.J. told her to bring a CD Monday to the site so they wouldn't have to listen to Larry's stuff.

He walked her to the door with his hand poised at her back. Mandy liked that he was still gentlemanly in spite of her embarrassing social hiccup earlier.

It was past midnight. Her parents were in bed, and Marc wouldn't be showing up for a few more hours yet. Her heart pounded with every step that brought them closer to the front door, to that place where uncertainty hung in the air.

Within the protection of the two-story vestibule, she turned and faced him. His eyes shimmered into a smile. His hand slipped from her back and reached up along her naked shoulder sending icy pain into a liquid pleasure. Mandy's heart shot into outer orbit. What was he going to do? She blinked. His smile slowly faded into something driven and intense. His gaze slipped to her mouth.

"Mandy," his voice was almost a whisper. "I want to kiss you."

The scent of him swirled around her head. He leaned close, and her pounding heart nearly shattered against her ribs. Not from fear, no. This was A.J. She trusted him. Liked him. Respected him for treating her with such care. His breath mingled with hers, their lips so close, hers tingled with want.

"But I won't kiss you, Mandy, unless you want me to," he whispered against her mouth.

"I want," she managed, head spinning. Then his lips covered hers. He didn't wrap around her, just slid his warm hands up to her face and held her there, his kiss soft and gentle. Mandy's heart skyrocketed into a galaxy of fluttering stars. Her knees trembled and she reached up, her hands skimming his chest until they wrapped around his neck and locked. She'd never been kissed like this—under the rough hands of a skilled craftsman, building feelings inside of her she didn't know existed. She was ready to abandon herself until he eased back and the cool air on her lips, the kind but controlled look in his eyes told her the kiss was over.

chapter ten

Mandy was certain when she got dressed for work the next Monday morning she looked different. Like a woman. Her skin was radiant, her eyes gleaming in a perpetual smile.

She put on her bathing suit and boardshorts, then tugged on fresh white socks and her work boots. Her hair went in a ponytail on top of her head. *Yes,* she thought giving herself a final once over in her full length mirror, she looked like the woman she was.

Who are you kidding, she mused. The color was from her dissolving sunburn, not her date with A.J.

She quickly applied sunscreen to avoid repeating the sun scorch today.

It was always sticky after dates, creating this strange vibe that you couldn't see, but was thick, dense and not easily navigated nonetheless. Though she doubted A.J. would be anything other than charming and professional, she'd been out with enough guys to know you could never assume.

Thankfully, Marc hadn't asked her about the date. It allowed her the privacy she wanted and felt was necessary so that he didn't acquire the wrong impression of A.J. He was prone to exaggerate, and the last thing Mandy wanted was for A.J. to lose his job because of Marc's overactive imagination.

His scowl greeted her when she got in the cab of the truck. "I told you not to wear that again."

"Get over it." She shut the door. "Nobody else was bothered by it." Mandy buckled her seatbelt.

He let out a snort.

"I thought you weren't going to tell me what to do? What happened to 'You're a big girl'?"

"Okay, okay. Fine." He backed out the car in a screech that screamed he was still angry. Mandy changed the subject.

"So, how was your night out on the town with Sensei Larry?"

"Oh, man." Marc rubbed the beard he'd neglected to shave. "Lame."

"What? Lar losing his touch?"

"No, he's got the touch, that's not the problem."

"She was there again?" Mandy asked, floored by the news. "That girl?"

"Woman," Marc corrected. "That woman and her name's Samantha. Yeah, she was there, and they'd prearranged it."

"No!"

Marc nodded. "I'm screwed with the bet, for sure. I figured Larry as a holdout."

"I can't believe he spent two nights with the same woman."

"More than two. Thursday, Friday, and they made plans for this coming weekend." Marc shook his head. "It doesn't look like it'll be getting any better. He didn't even look at anybody else all night. It sucked."

"Marc!"

Marc sighed. "This means my days of learning the art

at the hands of a true master are probably over."

Mandy laughed. "If you wanted to learn from a master, you've been shadowing the wrong guy. A.J.'s the—" Mandy stopped.

"*A.J.'s what*?" His eyes shot to hers. "What, Mand? If he laid one hand on you, I'll run his fingers through the band saw."

"Marc, stop it. Nothing happened." She wanted to kick herself for running off at the mouth. "He's the most decent date I've been on. Seriously. Considerate, not in any way pushy. A real man."

Marc snorted. "Yeah, right."

"It's true. Whatever side of him you've seen at work or at those clubs you guys go to, was not the side he showed me last night."

"Of course not, you're his boss's daughter and his supervisor's sister. He's not stupid."

Mandy didn't like the doubt Marc was trying to plant in her mind. "Anyway, we're just friends. I don't feel that way about him."

"I didn't think so."

"How—how could you tell?"

"I've seen the way you light up around guys you like—like a searchlight."

"I do not." She crossed her arms, face and body flushing.

"All girls do. That's how we guys know whether or not to make moves."

"Like a lighthouse you mean," she scoffed. "You're hopeless." She doubted A.J. relied on such ridiculous, if not inconsistent signals. Certainly she hadn't been lit up like a lighthouse last night, had she?

"So," she started as they pulled into the Haynes parking lot. She saw the guys waiting in their shorts and shirts, coffee cups steaming in their hands. "Was I like that last night? Come on, Marc, the truth."

He was grinning and she hated that. He pulled the car into his spot and killed the engine then looked over. "You weren't megawatt. More like streetlamp." He got out and shut the door.

But there had been light inside, Mandy knew that, she'd felt it. It's what made her want to kiss A. J.

"Morning, baby doll." A.J.'s green eyes glittered over the rim of his coffee cup, sending a trickle of warmth down her middle. He had on denim work shorts and an orange shirt. No bandana. His hair was scruffy, like a brush with abused bristles. A charcoal hoodie was tucked under his arm. She walked over trailing Marc.

"Morning." She sent everyone a small wave, taking special notice of Boston, who stood shoulder-to-shoulder with A.J., his hands tucked in the front pockets of his khaki carpenter shorts. He wore a yellow tee shirt today, the color of the sun, and it made his skin darker, his eyes sharper. He looked kind of anxious, and Mandy wondered why.

"You bring your sunscreen today?" Boston asked. Mandy blinked, surprised. He usually took a good hour to warm up in the mornings.

"Yes." She nodded. "I did."

His sharp gaze slowly, purposefully raked the whole of her before returning to her face.

Mandy shivered. A.J. stepped forward and held out his hoodie. "You cold? Here. Take it."

Marc took one look at her and snatched the

hoodie, shoving it at her. "Yeah. Good idea."

A sudden chill sent goose bumps over Mandy's skin so she slipped it on. "Thanks. Come on, let's go," she said, and crawled into the truck bed. She plopped down, perturbed.

She brought her knees up and crossed her elbows, burying her head so she could think. Sort. Figure out. A.J. was handling what had happened between them with the smooth ease she had anticipated, and Boston had no idea what had gone on. Still, he seemed turbo-attentive. Maybe he did know what had happened last night, maybe the guys had been talking about it before she and Marc got there. That didn't sound right. Mandy didn't know any guys that discussed their dates except Larry and Marc, and they only reveled over conquests.

The truck swayed as everybody piled in. She heard the thud of steps near but didn't look to see who it was. If it was A.J. she'd talk to him just like she always did. If Boston had chosen to sit back here with her, she'd...Her heart skipped just thinking about him. Her palms went wet. Curiosity and hope mixed, and she lifted her head just as Marc started up the diesel engine.

Boston. He sat down next to her, his shoulder flush with hers. Mandy clutched her knees. Every cell, every nerve and fiber jumped from the strong pressure of his body next to hers.

The wild waves of his hair lifted and tangled in the wind as they drove. His profile was strong, determined and utterly mesmerizing. She could stare at him for hours, she realized, like an insipid idiot.

"How was your weekend?" he asked, bringing his knees up close enough so he could rest his arms on them.

His dark gaze sliced her open. He knew she'd spent time with A.J., was that what he was after?

"Good." She skipped Friday night's details. "My mom and I went shopping. She came home with a haul but I didn't find anything. Sunday we watched a golf tournament. Marc's addicted to any and all things sports. How was yours?"

He lifted a shoulder. "I fixed a clogged sink in unit two-A, changed a lock on a bedroom door in one-B."

"Ah, the joys of home ownership."

"Yeah," he chuckled, "right."

"So you basically went from work to work."

"Basically."

"No fun at all? Nothing for yourself?"

"Owner upkeep is fun in a round about way – keeps your investment competitive."

She laughed, leaning into his shoulder for a second. "You know what I mean. Everybody needs some down time. Workout time, bookstore time – whatever."

"I spent my free time at the bookstore."

"Yeah? Did you make some new discoveries?"

"No." The air rushed by and around them, loosening the shorter strands of Mandy's hair. She tried to spread them back, but they just whipped out again, catching Boston's keen gaze.

His eyes moved out over the horizon, at the mountains on the other side of the lake, at the sun just starting to spread light into the valley. "I used to go to the bookstore in search of something. But this time I knew what I wanted wasn't going to be there."

A knot formed in Mandy's throat. She didn't know what to say, wasn't sure what he meant, and didn't dare think he was speaking metaphorically.

"I always know what I want when I go," she said. She was sure her girlish fantasies were too ripe and twisted, and she needed to get back to reality. "I've memorized the home improvement section, so I know what's there. I know what I've read, what I want to read, and what I have to read to get me where I want to go."

He smiled. "That'd be you, yeah. Set your course and stay on it. How did you get so settled?"

"There's comfort in things conventional."

"True." He nodded, his smile dissolving into taut lines. "And security."

"You're kind of like that, aren't you? I mean, you study about ways to invest. You own a fourplex that you live in. You've got a great job, even if it's not your dream job. That's not a guy who throws caution to the wind."

He dipped his head a moment. "Not about financial things, that's for sure."

"Ah. But your heart's another story, right?"

When his eyes met hers, there was a flash of guilt and sorrow but also a fresh spark. "What about you?" he asked.

"Me?"

"Yeah, you and your heart."

She cleared her throat. "My heart pretty much travels the same, conventional road my life does."

"So you don't ever lose your head? Get swept up? Or tangled in anything?"

She shook her head. "Nope. Tangled doesn't fit into my plan."

He laughed. "That's good, I think."

"Cuts down on the drama, that's for sure," she said.

"Drama," he sighed.

"You sound like you're familiar with the term, and I'm pretty sure it's not because you were a thespian in high school."

"Not a thespian, just a bad judge of the opposite sex."

"Oh." He sounded so resigned. "Chronically?"

He laughed. "Not chronically. Recently. That's why I took that vow. I was sick of the drama, the games. The lies," his voice was hard.

Mandy nodded. The truck turned onto the empty stretch of road that led to the new housing developments, one of which was her father's *Homes by Haynes* block. She wasn't anxious to get there; she was enjoying the conversation too much, feeling like she was finally getting beyond the mystery. She'd only had carefully meted glimpses of this contemplative guy but what she was beginning to see was deep, gentle, sensitive and cautious to a fault, with a brittle temper.

"So you're giving yourself a break. I still think that's a smart idea. Wounds need time to heal." She heard him sigh and looked over in time to see frustration on his face. "Something wrong?"

He squinted, looking at the vacant lots as they drove by. "Yeah. Actually, there is."

"Having second thoughts about her?"

He shook his head, still not meeting her gaze. "No. That'll never be a problem again."

"Wow, must have been pretty nasty. I'm sorry."

When he looked at her, it wasn't with anything but truth. "I can tell that about you. I appreciate the honesty."

"Is it work? I can talk to Marc—"

"I don't think I can keep my vow."

Mandy's eyes opened wide just as the truck pulled to a stop. Dust blew up around the wheels, and circled in the air. She heard the doors of the cab open, but her gaze was fixed on Boston's face. There was no disguising what she saw coloring his eyes a deep, sober black, drawing his jaw into a knot. But her heart refused to believe it.

The guys got out of the cab. Mandy wished time would stop so she could continue her conversation with Boston, but Marc, Larry, and A.J. came around to the back of the truck.

Boston stood and held out a hand to her which she took before lifting to her feet.

"Don't think you can or don't want to?" she asked.

The hint of a smile was in his eyes. He leaned close enough that she knew he wanted to keep their discussion private. "That's what's cool about you. You say it like it is."

He turned and hopped down. Mandy stood statue-still in shock. Yeah, she said it like it was, *but what was it?*

He held his hand up for her and she grasped it, easing herself down into the middle of the guys, all waiting to get to the storage chest and unload their belts and other tools. The chance to talk any more was lost in the expedited steps of getting set up and starting work.

"Mand." Marc slipped the skill saw strap over his shoulder. "You work with A.J and Charlie on finishing the inside walls. When you get to the second bath, A.J. will show you how to frame in the tub and shower. Charlie, you can keep on keeping on with the interior walls of bedroom one and two."

Mandy nodded. Marc and Larry took off for the second floor. Larry's boombox hung from his right hand.

A.J. pulled his red bandana out of his pocket and wrapped it around his head, his green eyes crinkling into a smile. "Feeling better today, baby doll?"

Boston was still adjusting his tool belt, so Mandy was sure he heard the conversation, even though he was intently buckling. "Feeling fine, thanks."

"Had me worried Friday night." A.J. finished knotting the bandana. "You're a delicate little thing." He reached out a finger and traced it from her shoulder blade down to her wrist just in time for Boston to notice.

"Me?" Her laugh fluttered out.

"Yeah, you." A.J.'s smile deepened. "You can't be anymore than, what, a size three? That pretty little sundress you wore was something else." A.J.'s glittering expression was a mix of genuine pleasure and teasing. Boston looked like he was about ready to say something, but he didn't.

"Thanks, A.J. I'm glad you liked it."

A.J. started toward the house walking backwards. "Let's get to work." He jerked his head at the structure. Mandy glanced at Boston, catching the faintest twitch in his tight jaw before she followed A.J.

Upstairs the mood wasn't any more comfortable, and Larry's rough music seemed to stir the electric vibe into a frenzy. She started out with Boston in bedroom number three, framing in the walls and closet. Next to them, A.J. constructed the insides of bedroom number two.

Across the floor in the master bedroom, Marc and Larry laughed and hammered like usual, Larry denying his three nights and two days with Samantha meant anything, Marc lamenting over his loss of a guru even though he'd won the pot of money in the bet over Larry's women. Every now and then Mandy looked up and found A.J. glancing over, or caught Boston's gaze on her. Once, both men caught her at the same time, and she smiled and started to sweat.

"So," Mandy began because Boston hadn't said anything except work talk since they'd started. "What do you think of Larry's fall from grace?"

"Is that what it is?" His tone was wry.

"He spent the last three days with one woman, what would you call it?"

"That's about as fallen as it gets," A.J. said from a few feet away. The framed walls didn't allow for private conversations.

"Sounds like it to me." Mandy shot a nail into a stud to secure the middle support.

A.J. finished one section of wall and started on the next. "You admitting defeat, Larry?" he called.

Larry looked over and lifted his shoulders. "Can't help it, man. I know when I've been had."

"Lucky dog," Marc scowled.

Mandy enjoyed the light teasing. "What are you complaining about? You won the pot. What's she like, Lar?"

Larry didn't say anything, so Marc piped, "Oh, baby. Hotter than a XR."

"So you think this is it?" Mandy asked. "The real

thing?"

"Heck no." Larry laughed and Marc joined in. "But it's good enough for now."

Mandy frowned and caught Boston watching her.

"What?" he asked, voice low enough that Marc and Larry wouldn't hear. She wasn't sure about A.J., he was just on the other side of the framed-in wall.

"It's just so shallow."

Boston centered a piece of wood in the frame. "Yeah, it is. But maybe she's just as shallow."

"True. I can't see Larry with anybody too deep, that would be like trying to build a foundation on sand—you can't do it."

Boston looked over, studied her. "You're right. But I don't think Larry's after something sturdy."

She was glad they were talking. She liked hearing his take on things. The sun was creeping toward noon and the heat was intensifying. Sweat beaded at the sides of his face.

"Sometimes it's not about sturdy," A.J. said. Mandy and Boston looked through the wood slats at him, a few feet away, kicking sawdust from where he was standing. "Sometimes it's just about having a good time." He looked at Boston. "Right?"

"As long as it's fair," Boston said.

"Oh," A.J. chuckled. "I don't play any other way."

One corner of Boston's lip lifted. "Neither do I."

"I'm glad you two are thoughtful that way," Mandy interjected. "I don't know any woman who starts into a relationship hoping to get used and tossed like a Dixie cup."

A.J.'s teeth sparkled. "You know just the right things

to say, don't you, baby doll." He backed to the wall he was working on. "That's what makes you adorable."

Mandy took the flattery with a tilt of her head and a smile. "Thank you." Suddenly, the air steamed. She fanned her face with both hands and closed her eyes. "Whew, it's getting hot. Don't you think it's getting hot?"

"Heat never bothered me," A.J.'s comment was easy, just like his shrug.

Boston sauntered back to the wall they were in the middle of constructing. "I do my best work in the heat."

Mandy's wide eyes flicked from one man to the other. "Think I'll get a drink. Either of you want one?"

"I'll take a water." A.J. resumed work.

"You?" Mandy waited for Boston's gaze to meet hers. He shook his head.

Mandy headed downstairs. Surely this couldn't be about her. It seemed ridiculous, yet she'd seen enough soap operas, read enough books, and even some of her friends had been caught in the middle of triangles the likes of Bermuda. In the middle of the taut frenzy just wasn't somewhere she ever thought she'd find herself.

She took two bottles back up, wondering if the sticky mood would still be there.

"Thanks." A.J took a bottle. He'd taken off his shirt while she was gone and slung it over the ledge of a framed-in window. His gaze swept her shoulders, then her legs before slowly coming up to her face. "You're getting nice color."

"Am I?" She held her arms out and peered. "Finally."

"Why is it women think they have to be tan?" he asked.

"I don't know. For me, it's this battle I've had with

the sun since I was a little kid. Like I have to prove I can be something other than red. Or white. I can tan." She laughed.

"I figured it wasn't about being like every other sun worshipper out there." A.J. screwed the lid back on his bottle. "You're too smart for that."

"If I was smart, I'd give the sun the victory and wave a white towel. I can't help it, though. I like the heat. It makes me feel good."

The light in A.J.'s eyes darkened, sending a twist of something fast and hot down her gut. "Heat stays with you," he said, voice raspy. "Leaving its brand, right?"

"Leaving its burn is more like it." Boston came up beside her, challenge in his eyes aimed first at A.J. then sliding to her. "But then you're smart enough to wear plenty of protection."

"Of course she is," A.J. said. "She can take care of herself."

"I know when to get in the shade," Mandy put in, on the verge of laughing at the simile the three of them were tossing around like a beach ball.

Boston wiped the hem of his shirt over his face. "Sometimes the shade's not even safe enough." When their eyes met, he crossed his arms and tugged his shirt up and over his head, keeping her gaze locked with his.

Mandy's heart bounced at the provocative move. She tingled when he bunched his tee shirt between his hands, staring unblinkingly at her.

"I think we stopped talking about the ill effects of sun exposure about fifteen seconds ago," she squeaked. Boston grinned and A.J. broke out in a warm laugh.

Mandy held out her hand. "Let me fold that for you."

The black flecks in Boston's eyes flickered. Mandy felt the touch of his skin reach out and warm her all the way to her toes when he handed her the shirt. Rather than move away so she had the distance she needed to fold it, she turned just enough so she could shake the shirt out, then folded it neatly into a square before handing it back.

"Thank you."

"No problem."

"Baby doll."

Mandy tore her gaze away from Boston and looked at A.J. He ticked his head toward the room they were supposed to frame next. "Let's get to work in this bathroom." He winked.

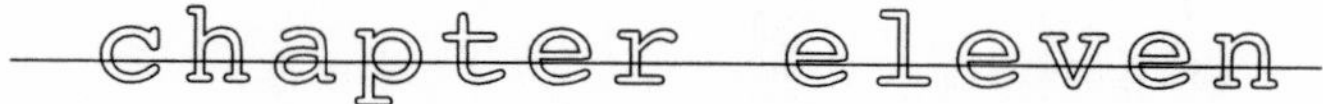

For lunch they piled into the truck and headed into town. Mandy argued that, since she'd missed on Friday, it was her day to pick a dining spot. Marc grumbled at the use of the word *dining* and warned her that if she took them back to another bookstore, he'd make her eat wood chips.

"Besides," Marc eyed her, "You'll have to wait in the car. You can't go in any place looking like that."

"I'll throw on a company shirt!"

Mandy went purely with her craving: Taco Bell fit the budget and was close enough that they wouldn't spend the hour driving.

As with most fast food places during peak lunch hour, Taco Bell was no less crowded than the next place. Mandy took her Nacho Bellgrande and Pepsi and sat at the first empty table she could find.

A.J. joined her with his tray of five crispy tacos and giant soda. He slid into the Formica booth and sat across from her. "I like it when you pick."

"I had to have Taco Bell today."

A.J. tugged the paper sleeve off his straw. "Cravings are hard to ignore."

Something about the sandy tone in his voice made her throat go dry. She reached for her Pepsi. She watched Boston come to the table with his plastic bowl of taco salad and a bottle of water.

She eyed his food. "Don't you ever succumb?"

He sat next to her and their shoulders brushed. "To what?" He twisted the top off his water bottle and drank.

"To temptation, to eating what you feel like?"

"I do eat what I feel like," he grinned. "And, I've given in to temptation plenty in my life." He yanked the plastic sleeve off of his fork/spoon. "What about you, A.J.?"

A.J.'s jaw churned. He swallowed. "You betcha." His eyes sparkled with teasing. "Bet you don't, though do ya, baby doll?"

"Are you kidding?"

"What tempts you?"

Mandy's cheeks flushed. Over A.J.'s shoulder, Marc and Larry took their orders to an empty table on the other end of the dining room. "Food," she said, then popped a corn chip laden with cheese and meat into her mouth.

"And books?" Boston asked.

"And books. Boring, huh. Safe though, and I've always liked safe."

"You keep it like that and you'll stay out of trouble." A.J. picked up his second taco.

"Trouble doesn't hold any fascination for me."

"Not even a little bit?" The twinkle in A.J.'s eyes was gone, something curious replaced it, and Mandy swallowed a thick knot down with a gulp of Pepsi.

"Well." She took a deep breath, suddenly warm from head to toes. "Okay, there's that romantic mystique of trouble. The kind that really isn't dangerous. That's trouble I can fantasize about, maybe even get into."

"Sounds interesting."

A laugh fluttered out of Mandy. "Yeah, well, that's about all I'd do – fantasize.

Marc got in enough real trouble for us both."

Both A.J and Boston laughed. "He's a guy." A.J. crunched on the taco. "Guys are prone to crashing."

"You're better off," Boston said. Mandy thought she heard admiration in his tone. "Trouble's overrated."

"Come on," A.J. said. "Trouble's how you learn. It's like a spice. You gotta have a little to flavor life."

"Yeah, well, some spices I can deal with, others I can't," Boston said.

"Charlie?" The high pitched voice had them all looking up into the face of a tall, leggy woman with a mane of black hair.

Mandy looked at Boston, who'd gone still next to her, his eyes wide. "Alexis."

It didn't take a genetic specialist to figure out that this tall, dark vixen was the one who had shredded Boston's heart. The woman flipped her black hair over a tanned shoulder. Behind her stood a blonde man who looked like she'd just fished him out of the sea. All that was missing was his surfboard and swim trunks.

"You on break from work?" she asked, sweeping everyone at the table with her amused gaze.

"Yeah." Boston didn't look at her again, focusing instead on the taco salad sitting in front of him.

After a thick moment of silence, she flashed her teeth. "I'm Alexis."

A.J. half stood and extended his hand. "A.J."

"Mandy," Mandy said.

"This is Eric." She wrapped her arms around Neptune standing next to her, and nuzzled a kiss against his neck.

Boston extended an eager hand toward Eric. "How's it going?" Mandy had to steal a peek at Boston's face. His voice was so chipper; she wondered what had suddenly gotten into him.

Alexis, too, seemed taken aback by his cordiality. Eric shook Boston's hand.

Then Boston sat back and slid his arm around Mandy, bringing her in close. His palm caressed her shoulder in an intimate move that fired a flush through Mandy's body. Mandy's eyes widened, her heart pounded.

Alexis eyed her, her brows shooting up in shock. "Are you two…?"

"Yeah, we are." Boston wrapped his arm more tightly around Mandy's shoulder and quickly leaned over and kissed her cheek. Alexis blinked in what Mandy thought was shock, but Mandy was trying to settle her own bubbling surprise. For a second, her gaze met A.J.'s. His chewing had stopped and his usually teasing smile had vanished.

"I didn't know you were dating anybody." Alexis wrapped her arm tighter around the arm of the beach god standing next to her.

Mandy was a turbulence of shock, anger and disappointment. She didn't like being used. At the same time she'd seen Boston's hurt and his resolve to get over this woman. She wasn't sure how to respond.

She snuggled next to him, trailing a finger down the side of his neck. "He's private about our relationship," she began. "That's one of the things I like about him. Private and protective. Makes me feel lucky."

Boston's dark eyes met hers and for a second, the

reality of what was happening flashed, along with other emotions Mandy couldn't read and she wasn't sure she wanted to. If he was going to use her, he'd better be cool with what she did. Questions later.

Still, her insides trembled being that close to him, touching him that way, smelling his skin so near she could almost taste it. To kiss him in front of this loser who had hurt him, that would teach her something, wouldn't it?

"Wow." Alexis's surprise was obvious on her face, and she didn't like what she was seeing. Mandy smiled with satisfaction. Then she turned Boston's chin and brought his face close. His breath fanned hot and static against her lips. Anticipation turned his brown eyes a darker shade. She leaned close.

Her lips met his. She closed her eyes and let their mouths melt. His heat became her heat, his taste her taste. His lips responded, shock discarded by urgency, shooting tingling fire from her mouth to every nerve in her body. At her shoulder, his fingers gripped hard and then his other hand slid around her waist and tugged her closer.

Time vanished. Sound disappeared. What began as an act was now real, warm and so lovely Mandy slipped her arms around his neck barely conscious of anything but the thrill streaming through every part of her.

A.J.'s cough startled her, Boston too, because he jerked back. Dazed, Mandy hardly noticed when he eased her arms away, looking at her in a moment taut with puzzlement. Mandy was certain she saw anger flickering in his dark eyes before they shifted back to Alexis who now stood with her hand on her hip, her brow raised over a smirk.

"My, well," Alexis said, tone frosty. "I thought you hated public displays of affection."

"He wasn't with the right woman," Mandy said, taking Boston's hand and holding it on top of the table.

Alexis's gaze flicked there.

Alexis lifted her chin and drew her man next to her. "Come on, let's go. I'd rather eat somewhere else. It was nice to meet you, A.J." She glanced at him, then her cold eyes met Mandy's. "I forgot your name."

"*Mandy*."

Alexis merely stared then turned her disproving gaze to Boston. "See ya, Charlie."

"Yeah."

Mandy watched Alexis and her companion go out the door. "Guess she lost her appetite." Mandy turned back around. A.J.'s face was stony. She had Boston's hand tightly in hers, and she glanced at it before releasing it and picking up her fork. Boston stared at his untouched taco salad. The corners of his jaw were rock hard. Mandy moved her chips around her container with the tines of the fork.

The silence was as suffocating as wood dust, and almost as unbearable. Mandy looked at A.J., whose expression was not amused. What? She'd only played along. In her mind, if anyone should be peeved, it should be her—being used like some cheap skank for the sake of…what? If it was revenge Boston was after, he sure didn't look satisfied. Over A.J.'s shoulder, her gaze caught on Marc and Larry, grinning like two cats that had just swallowed bluebirds. They slapped palms. Mandy's skin burned.

They stood, laughing and talking, then threw their

trash away before coming to the table.

"You caved, dude." Marc grinned at Boston, who looked thoroughly miserable, Mandy thought.

The momentary confusion on Boston's face shifted to understanding. He sat forward and dragged his hands down his face. Mandy wasn't sure why she felt the need to defend him, especially after he'd used her like that and not yet said a word about it. But she'd willingly participated in the little charade, and Marc and Larry deserved to know that the scene was just that—a charade.

"It was nothing," she said, picking up a now soggy corn chip. "He's still…clean."

Marc laughed. "That's what it looked like, yeah. You're full of it."

"I'm serious, Marc."

"She's right," Boston's tone was sharp, and it cut straight through Mandy's confused heart. He stood, picked up his untouched taco salad, his body twitching like a racehorse at the gate. "That kiss was nothing."

Mandy's heart fell to her feet. She couldn't believe he'd said the words.

Marc and Larry caught the hard shift in Boston's demeanor and their smiles

flattened. Marc stuffed his hands in his pockets. Mandy recognized the fury building in her brother's face all tight and turning red, and her neck broke out in a sweat.

"Then what were you doing with her?" Marc hissed.

Mandy shot to her feet. "It wasn't what it looked like. That chick at the table was—"

"Mandy, stop." Boston's eyes flashed to hers and

held. Then he looked at Marc. "It's really none of your business." He stepped over to the trash receptacle, shoved his untouched taco salad through the swinging door, and left the restaurant.

Marc grabbed Mandy's elbow. "What was that all about?"

She had to temporarily ignore her tender heart and bruised ego, it just wouldn't do for Marc to see that Boston's cold detachment was affecting her. She tugged her elbow free and scowled. "None of your business."

Mandy dumped her trash and followed Boston outdoors into the noon sun. His stride was fast and frustrated as he headed toward the truck. She wasn't sure she should confront him, but the way he'd looked into her eyes and said that the little charade had been nothing stuck with her like a bee stinger she couldn't pluck out.

"Hey." She finally caught up with him and they strode shoulder-to-shoulder. When he looked over, even though it was only for a moment, her heart fluttered. "You want to talk about that?"

He stopped at the back of the truck and slammed his hands on the tailgate. A heavy sigh seeped from his chest. He shook his head, his gaze off over the parking lot. Then his black eyes locked on hers, sending a cold shudder down her middle. "Not now." He pulled himself up and over the tailgate and sat down.

Incensed, Mandy opened her mouth to lay into him for using her when she heard Marc, Larry and A.J.'s voices. They were coming out of Taco Bell and heading for the truck. She was numb inside.

She climbed over the tailgate and plopped down

directly across from Boston, satisfied when he looked at her with surprise on his face. "That kiss wasn't nothing," she kept her voice low. If he thought she was going to let this go and cower away like some spineless female, he had another thing coming.

"I said not now," he said between teeth.

It was juvenile to glare at him, even though she was swimming in conflicting feelings. She took a deep breath, pondering what to do. For now she'd respect his wishes and not pry it out of him. The last thing she wanted was for Marc to suspect anything, anyway.

Marc and Larry were talking about Larry's date with Samantha as they got into the truck cab. A.J. hopped over the back of the bed and sat himself down next to her, his arm brushing hers when he crossed them over his chest. He stretched out his legs.

Boston's narrowed gaze honed in on the zero distance between her and A.J., but Mandy wasn't sure why. If he cared at all that she'd kissed him and made a fool out of herself all in the name of helping him out of a jam, he wasn't showing it.

"You okay?" A.J. asked before Marc started the truck and the diesel engine grumbled.

Mandy nodded, casually keeping Boston out the corner of her eye. He was still watching them like a hawk. It gave her a small wince of satisfaction.

They didn't speak during the fifteen minute drive to the site. Mandy tried not to let frustration push her into behaving like an idiot and using A.J. to make Boston jealous. Boston's gaze was locked on how close A.J. had planted himself next to her—something she found interesting, but not satisfying. She couldn't interpret what

Boston was thinking behind his dark eyes.

At the site, Boston jumped out of the truck the minute Marc killed the engine. A.J. stood and held out a hand to Mandy who took hold and rose to her feet. But when she stepped toward the tailgate, A.J. held her hand firm and brought her flush with him, his green eyes sharp staring into hers. "What are you doing, baby doll?"

Mandy's throat closed. He was so near, so very strong holding her hand as firm as a bear. Anger, frustration and confusion seemed to tighten his every muscle standing close enough to her that she wanted to take a step back but A.J.'s fast tug on her hand told her he meant business.

"I'm not talking about getting out of the truck," A.J.'s voice dropped because Marc and Larry were rounding the vehicle and Mandy felt the guys watching even though they went about getting their tools out of the chest.

Mandy swallowed jittering nerves. "I was helping Boston out of a jam."

A.J.'s eyes stayed locked on hers and so did his hand, wrapped around hers. He seemed to consider her words as he stood there still as a statue. A shudder rambled deep inside of Mandy aware now that the guys weren't talking anymore but loitering at the back of the truck, listening. Boston's dark form moved into her peripheral vision.

A.J.'s grip softened and he rubbed her hand with both of his in a caress. Then he led her to the open truck bed, jumped down and held up a hand for her again.

Mandy stole a glimpse of Boston, belted up, watching. She set her hand in A.J.'s and let him assist her.

"I want to get the second floor interior walls done by tonight," Marc said. Mandy thought his voice broke the tension strung between her, A.J., and Boston, and she let out a sigh as she reached into the toolbox and retrieved her belt.

But the minute Larry and Marc headed into the house, the blaze of pressure was back, flames of frustration and confusion leaping all around them.

"You want to work with me, baby doll?" A.J. asked, slipping his red bandana around his head.

"She and I work together first." Boston's tone was hard, his glare aimed at A.J. "That's the protocol."

A thin smile slit A.J.'s lips. He finished tying the knot at the back of his head. "I don't know Charlie, you seem to lose your head when it's convenient for you. Kinda unprofessional."

In a fast step, Boston was chest-to-chest with A.J. who stood with his fists flexing at his side.

Mandy swallowed and took a tentative step toward the two men. "It'll be fine, A.J. I'll start with Boston. He's right."

"I don't know how *right* he is," A.J. said, locked in a stare with Boston. Boston snickered and A.J.'s gaze slid to Mandy. "But you're calling the shots here."

Mandy's eyes widened when both men looked at her.

"Hey!" Marc's booming voice called from the upstairs of the house. He stood at the open stairway watching. "Let's get to work."

A.J. sent him a grin and a salute. "On our way, boss." He crossed between Mandy and Boston, his cool gaze lingering on Mandy.

Boston's hands sat on his tool belt. He looked restless. Mandy wanted to talk about what was going on, what had happened, but realized the timing was off for that. First and foremost they had a job to do.

She followed Boston's dusty steps into the house. White Snake blared from Larry's boombox in a corner. A.J. went to work in the bathroom they'd framed earlier, and he put the finishing touches on the tub and shower framing. Mandy trailed Boston to the closet they were going to construct in one of the three bedrooms.

"What the heck is this?" Marc's boom cannonballed through Larry's loud music and every hammer and nail gun went silent. Marc stood next to a wall in bedroom two that Boston and Mandy had worked on earlier.

"There's supposed to be a window here," he barked. Boston started over, so Mandy followed. Mistakes like this weren't uncommon during framing. Her dad had told her stories of every kind of building error from a house being feet off its intended foundation to stairs going up the wrong side of a room.

"I want this fixed." Marc looked at Boston as if the mistake was his fault. Boston seemed to accept the chastisement.

He nodded. "Same size as the other one?"

Marc looked at the other window in the room, crossed to it and whipped out his measuring tape before he stepped back with a nod. "Yeah."

"Should we check the blueprint?" Mandy asked.

Marc scowled. "If window A is thirty-five by thirty-five,

it's a pretty good bet window B is the same. But, yeah, check it out, Mand." Then he went back to work.

Mandy joined Boston at the wall where the window was supposed to be. "I guess we should have seen it. It's an obvious place for a window, look at the view. It's so clear. You can see everything from here."

Boston didn't agree or disagree, he just started in working. Mandy found the blueprint and double checked before joining Boston again. His tone was sharp and direct as he gave her orders. Mandy bristled. She didn't mind being instructed, but being told what to do was another story. When they stood together as she held the two-by-fours for him to hammer in place, she couldn't bear the strain a moment longer.

"So what happened at lunch?" she asked.

His palms wrapped around the wood so close to hers, she felt the heat of his hands. Barely two feet of space stood between them and his scent mixed with the smell of the raw wood surrounding them. His brown eyes looked into hers but he didn't say anything.

"You one of those guys that doesn't like to talk about stuff that's uncomfortable?" she asked.

He positioned the wood. "Hold this," he said. She did, still glaring at him. He dropped down in a squat, securing the wood below and Mandy's glare softened at the site of his lovely crown. She shook her head and looked away. She had to stay firm.

He stood and his expressive eyes seemed to overflow with determination. "I'm one of those guys who like to talk about stuff that's private in private."

Mandy swallowed a lump. "Oh. Well. What was that at lunch then? That kiss wasn't very private."

His face flushed a shade of red but he held her gaze.

She glanced over at A.J. a good twenty feet away. Marc and Larry were across the floor. "This private enough?"

"Not for me."

"It is for me. I want to know why you said that kiss was nothing. That hurt."

Boston's dark eyes averted to the floor. He set his hands on his hips and let out a quiet sigh before looking at her again. "I'm sorry. That wasn't…it was all I could think of to say at the moment."

"I was going off your cue, for your information," Mandy lowered her voice even though frustration rode it. "I thought that's what you wanted—to make her jealous."

Boston took a deep breath, studying her. "Yeah. That's what I *thought* I wanted."

"So what's wrong? Nothing was compromised. You're still clean—"

"—It's not about the bet."

"Well then, I'm pretty sure Diva Alexis got the message. In fact, she was green when she left, I saw her skin turn, I swear." Mandy let out a laugh hoping Boston would smile—laugh—anything, but his stoic expression remained, in fact, he looked ridden with guilt.

"I've never done anything like that before," he said, voice quiet. "I'm not a game player. I hate it, in fact."

He'd told her that before. Mandy hated that she'd helped him do something he found distasteful. What was worse, she wasn't one to engage in games either. Why had they both fallen into something neither liked, and with each other? Other important issues pressed on

Mandy's mind.

"Why did you want to make her jealous? I thought you said you'd moved on."

He seemed to try to figure out the answer right there on the spot, and he shifted with discomfort. "I don't know. I saw her climb all over him and...it got under my skin. I was angry. It was like all of her crap came back at me, like I was being used like some toy again. I hated it."

"So you played right back...with your own toy. Me."

His gaze met hers. Mandy's heart was dangerously close to bruising. Suddenly, A.J. was standing next to them. His cough startled them both. Mandy was frustrated at the interruption. Boston hadn't answered her and she wanted to know if he still had feelings for that woman.

A.J. rocked back on his heels, looked from Boston to her with an expression of curiosity mixed with what Mandy was sure was annoyance. "I need you now, baby doll."

Mandy gave him a nod. "Sure." In her tender heart, she wished Boston would take hold of her arm, pull her over and press her back into the framed wall they'd just erected. She wished he'd kiss her and whisper along her cheek that she was who he wanted. Alexis was over. He'd wanted that kiss.

Mandy kicked at some fallen wood scraps as she crossed to where A.J. worked. The space of the shower/tub was getting more cramped as wood filled in. A.J. pointed out what he'd left for her: the arched framing around the door.

His shoulder brushed hers as he instructed how to install the small pieces of wood that would secure the archway in place. Because the wood was curved and large, the job would be easier with two sets of hands rather than one, he said.

She held an end up over her head and realized she'd need the small step ladder so she could hold it in place.

"It's over there, baby doll." With a nod, A.J. gestured in the direction of where a small step ladder sat propped against the framing. Mandy jogged over to it, stealing a glance at Boston who was framing and didn't look at her. Because he didn't, she felt a pinch inside.

Part of her wanted to pinch him back. But she didn't know if he even cared about her that way. His heart was probably still beating for that Alexis chick, so some jealous play would be a waste of time. She had just told him she didn't play those games, so why would she start now?

She wondered if this was just the way of it in the adult world. She set the ladder down and climbed. A.J. handed her one end of the arched wood while he held the other.

"Hold it steady there." A.J. placed his end flush with the wood pieces trimmed for support. "What's on your mind, Mandy?"

He so rarely used her name, and Mandy couldn't help but look at him. He hammered in a nail, then met her curious gaze.

"How did you know I was thinking about something?"

"You had that look about you."

So what if he'd chosen not to sit behind a desk, he was smart in the human ways that count. "You've been trained well, A.J."

He chuckled, hammered in another nail, and

moved onto the next spot. "Four sisters will do that to a guy."

Mandy wondered if Boston had any sisters. The way he'd used her, she doubted he'd had a heads-up in the female department.

"Talk to me," A.J. said.

She wondered at the wisdom of sharing her thoughts about what had happened at lunch and her subsequent discussion with Boston. One glance at Boston, ignoring her, and her pride prickled. "I don't know…I just thought I was helping him out, you know? Showing that witch he was over her. But…he…" Mandy swallowed a hard lump of acceptance lodged in her throat. "I guess it didn't do what I thought it would."

A.J. let the hammer fly again, hard enough that Mandy jolted. He stood back and his steely green eyes met hers. "You're wrong about that, baby doll."

"What…" Mandy's heart fluttered. "You think it worked?"

"Oh, I think it worked just fine." A.J. moved closer now, as he focused on the center of the arch. "Hold it up. Steady."

Mandy's arms began to ache but she held the piece fast. A.J. positioned a nail and the muscles in his arms and shoulders turned to rock as he pounded it in. A slow coil wound tight in Mandy's stomach watching his strong arms.

"How do you know?" she asked, her voice low so their conversation stayed between them. Boston, she noticed, finally glanced over. A thread of satisfaction dangled inside of her when his gaze lingered.

"I know men." A.J. positioned another nail, this

one in the very center of the arch. His arms were lifted and Mandy caught a glimpse of the dark hair under his armpits. Musky sweat mixed with dirt and wood, and snuck into her nose but she didn't mind. In fact, she couldn't deny the calm feeling that had settled in her just talking to A.J. He was so wise, so much older, she appreciated that she could tell him anything and he understood.

"I bet you don't play games, do you?" she asked.

He plucked another nail from the leather bag hanging on his tool belt and moved closer. Mandy looked down into his aqua green eyes, so clear, so...mesmerizing. Warmth spread through her as his lips lifted into a grin. He'd kissed her with those lips, and she'd liked it. Liked the way his hands had expertly framed her face, the way his masculinity had made her feel so feminine.

A low chuckle rumbled from his chest. "Games? I suppose we've all been guilty of playing games."

"Even you?"

"Sure. There's a time when you think that's what a woman expects and playing a part is easier than being who you are."

He was right. "Is that time between the ages of fourteen and twenty nine?"

"I'm not sure when it ends." He laughed. "For some, I don't think it ever does." He looked over at Larry and Mandy followed his gaze, then gave a quick nod.

"Yeah, I gotcha there."

His gaze was sober. "You don't like playing, do you?"

"No. Is it obvious?"

"Not if you asked me at lunch. You looked like a pro at lunch. But I can tell now—here—games aren't for you."

"So..." How lame to ask a man for advice about another man. She was old enough to figure this out for herself.

"So now you don't know what move to make next." A.J. observed. He seemed to stare deep into her soul. Mandy took a deep breath. He stepped closer, his head at her chest. Mandy's heart banged against her ribs. The last time he'd been this close, he'd kissed her. Of course he wouldn't do that now, not here, but the fantasy flashed anyway, complete with Boston storming over and ripping them apart.

Heat flushed Mandy's skin, and a smile crept onto her face. A.J.'s gaze fell to her lips. Then he reached out and light as a gentle breeze, his calloused fingers skimmed her cheek. "You're something special, baby doll. Don't forget that."

His touch sent an electric current through her. Her insides nearly melted. Why did her body respond to his words, his touch, like a kitten to its master? She wanted to rub against him and curl up in his arms in total safety.

But she wasn't a kitten, she wasn't a baby, and since she couldn't understand why she was so drawn to him when her heart was also drawn to Boston. She tried to ignore the oozy way A.J. made her feel.

Movement out the corner of her eye took her attention to Boston. He stood eight feet away, his arms folded, brows knit tight over narrowed eyes.

A long quiet strung the three of them together and the slanted rays of the afternoon sun beating through the framed house heated the moment. Mandy was still standing on the step ladder, so she slowly descended. A.J. stuck out his hand to help her and she instinctively took hold of it. Boston shifted his feet.

"You ready for me now?" she asked Boston. He didn't say anything for what dragged out as another long moment, but held her gaze as if considering her words metaphorically.

A.J. touched her shoulder. Mandy watched Boston's gaze jerk there for the second the contact lasted. "We're done with the arch. It looks great, baby doll."

"Thanks, A.J."

With a light whistle, A.J. sauntered back to work on his own.

Mandy lifted her chin. "So…are you ready for me now?"

"Yeah, I am," Boston's voice was quiet but firm. He turned and headed back to the closet they'd been framing.

He pushed a two-by-four her direction and she took it, but he didn't let it go. He stood close, his eyes burning into hers like the fire of the sun. "He's too old for you," he whispered on a growl.

"Excuse me?"

"How—why—what are you doing with him, anyway?"

"I'm sure that's not any of your business."

His fingers were whitening around the two-by-four. "You're right, it's not. I'm—Can't you see what he's doing?"

"See what?" Mandy's spine prickled. "He's a gentleman. He's mature. He doesn't play games."

Boston let out a sneer. "Yeah, uh-huh. He's playing right now, Mandy. He's playing with you."

"And that makes him worse than you who played

with me, what, just a couple of hours ago?"

Boston stepped back, silenced. His tongue swept his lips in an itchy gesture that seemed to course through the rest of his body. "I said I was sorry about that."

"But you never explained yourself."

"I told you, I didn't—I couldn't—Seeing her set me back. That's all."

"You never answered my question."

His gaze averted as if he was uncomfortable, hated the question, and didn't want to answer her. A.J.'s soft whistle muddled the air, mixing with the far off boom of Guns 'n Roses coming from Larry's CD player.

Boston closed the distance between them. Mandy blinked. Her breath quickened in her chest. "I don't feel that way about her anymore." His gaze skimmed her face, finally stopping at her lips. "If that's what you want to know."

The hard knot in Mandy's throat went down with a swallow. "Oh. Well. That's good. Good for you."

"Yeah." Why she still saw stress drawing his fine features taut, Mandy couldn't fathom.

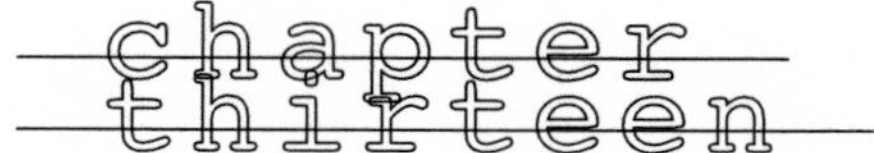

There was only one place Mandy knew of that could suck out the stress lodged in her stomach, and that was the bookstore. After work, she hurried home, showered, ate and changed.

All the while her mind was troubled with Boston. They'd kept their discussion work-related until the day was over. He'd been quiet but not cold. He'd said goodbye when they had all parted ways at the main office. She'd even caught him watching her as she got into the truck with Marc to head home.

A.J. had watched her too. In fact, he'd more than watched, he'd walked with her to the truck, opened the door for her, and given her another one of his you're-the-most-special-girl-on-the-face-of-the-planet looks.

Mandy's heart pulled in two directions.

She bowled into Barnes and Noble on a deep, cleansing breath and the scent of paper and coffee unwound her twisted image of Boston and A.J. This was just what she needed, to clear her head with a mocha freeze and stuff her nose into some architecture books.

She strode directly to the lounge area, her heart beating fast anticipating seeing Boston's dark mop of hair somewhere but the area was surprisingly empty. Only the kissing couple was there, sharing the LoveSac. She scanned the couch, saw Cam's backpack and smiled. Calm settled over her.

She found him hunkered down in the romance aisle, engrossed in a book with four others stacked at his side where he sat.

Quietly she approached, nearly bursting into a fit of giggles that he was so intense he didn't notice her. She stood close and utterly still.

"Whatcha reading, big guy?"

He almost jumped to his feet. "Crap, you scared me. And you interrupted a very hot scene."

"Sorry, just wanted you to know I was here." Mandy's gaze skimmed the lurid titles surrounding her. The spines of most of the books were obscene. Fascinated and repulsed, she couldn't stop her curious gaze magnetically fastened to the hundreds of books before her.

Cam rose to his feet, stuffing the stack under one arm while he held open the other book and continued to devour the contents. Mandy looked at the title of the book, *Three for the Money*.

"Three for the Money?"

Cam nodded, his eyes locked on the page. "Can you imagine the plot?"

"Do I want to?"

"Yeah babe."

"Want a drink?" she asked, guiding him out of the way of an oncoming woman who was also searching the aisle.

"Uh, yeah. My usual. You go get them. That guy's working the counter and I can't deal with it."

"You go save our couch." With that she gave him a light shove in the direction of the lounge and watched him narrowly escape walking head on into a bookshelf and another patron before he finally looked to see where he was going.

Mandy felt better already. With a grin on her face she headed for the café, her mouth watering for the specialty drink. She ordered, then headed back to the lounge area, frosty drinks in hand.

She stopped dead when her eyes lit on the tall, lean frame she'd spent the last few hours with. Boston stood browsing the new non-fiction titles, his back facing her. His legs looked even tanner against the baggy, ecru shorts he wore. She liked the pink and green striped polo shirt he had on, the color set his bronzed skin to an inviting, warm shade. A man who wore pink was a man she admired for self-confidence.

The turmoil she'd dumped at the door was back and wound tight in her stomach now. She didn't want to see him, didn't want him to see her. She wanted this bookstore night to be relaxing and fun, so she slid around the new arrivals display and ducked out of sight behind the bargain books shelves on her way back to the lounge area.

With a sigh, she plopped down next to Cam. Without taking his eyes from the pages before him, he reached out. Mandy laughed and set the drink in his outstretched hand. "Nice to see you, too."

"I'm sorry, what?" He finally looked up. "Man that was intense. Phew." He closed the book and drank the entire sixteen ounce drink in one long slurp. He clutched his head with his hands, his face puckering. "Brain freeze." When it was over, he let out a pleasurable sigh. "Better than a cold shower."

"Don't be getting yourself all worked up now, big guy."

Cam turned red.

Mandy sipped her drink, enjoying the flavors. But her gaze darted behind the couch, out into the store, sure she'd see Boston.

Cam eyed her, then twisted around for a look. "Who are we seeing? That guy from work?"

"Boston."

"The look on your face tells me whatever is going on between you and him is far more interesting than any of my books." He set the novel aside. "What's up?"

"He's here. I saw him up front."

"Did he see you?"

Mandy shook her head, sipped.

"And you don't want him to?"

Mandy paused, then shrugged. "I don't know. Things have just been too random, you know?"

"No, I don't. Tell me. Is the triangle still in place?"

"Unfortunately, yes. Or it was until today at lunch. Now, it's more like a square."

"A square? That would indicate there are four people involved and that means coupling. Who's the fourth corner?"

"Boston's ex. She happened to show up at Taco Bell today when we were all eating lunch."

"Oooh." Cam situated himself against the pillows on the couch.

"She was there with her new guy and Boston freaked about it. He put his arm around me, to—you know—make her jealous, and then I kissed him. And he kissed me back."

"What?!" Cam's voice ricocheted off the walls. What few patrons there were nearby looked over. Kissing couple broke their lip lock long enough to shoot a disparaging glare at them. Cam brought his legs up on the couch in a crossed-leg position and leaned close to her. "Why didn't you tell me?"

"I've been at work," Mandy whispered.

"You're supposed to text me with juice. This is huge! You guys are going to get married now."

Mandy rolled her eyes. "It wasn't like that. It was an act, that's all."

"An act of pure, raw, physical attraction. See? I told you. You put two alpha males out in the hot sun with one female and things are going to sizzle."

Mandy set down her drink with a plunk. "Nothing burned but my ego, Cam. That's the problem. He told me it was nothing, the kiss."

Cam's wide eyes grew round with concern. His mouth fell open. "He did not."

"He did. Here I was, playing off his cue, trying to help him show that witch he was over her and he tells me it didn't mean anything. It was lame. I felt like an idiot."

"That's wrong." Cam's freckled skin was turning pink. His head jerked around as he searched the store. "Where is this loser?"

Mandy slapped her hand on his arm. "Forget it. I should have known better."

"The turd deserves to have his brains knocked around."

"Forget it, Cam. I have to work with him, remember? I need to be professional. That's the problem, I didn't keep it professional."

"And he did when he put his arm around you? Snake."

"In his defense, he said he was out of sorts seeing his ex with another guy."

"So he uses you? No guy does that, Mand. That's low. Serpent low."

Mandy let out a sigh. But Cam hadn't seen the remorse on Boston's face, either. Remorse Mandy wasn't sure was aimed at the impromptu act or at his separation from Alexis.

"What about this other guy?" Cam asked. "P.J.?"

"A.J. He's still around."

"Did he see all this go down at Taco Bell?"

"Yeah, he was there. He didn't like it. He got all... protective."

A grin spread on Cam's face. "Now you're talking. I like this guy, A.J. Sounds like a real man."

Ooze slithered through Mandy's bones thinking about A.J. and his rough appeal. She sipped but barely tasted her drink. "He's a man all right."

Cam leaned close, all eyes and ears. "What? Tell me."

Mandy lifted a shoulder. She couldn't stop the grin from spreading her lips wide. "I can talk to him, you know? He's not into games and stuff. I like that."

"Games are for goons," Cam said with another scan around the place. "That Boston dude needs to read some romance and get it down right."

"Not his style."

"Obviously. I bet he's a non-fiction fool."

Mandy didn't like that she felt defensive for Boston. She should be agreeing with Cam. "Only in the self-improvement sense of the genre."

"Self-improvement? Obviously he doesn't comprehend what he's reading."

"Cam, forget it. I can take care of this mess. It's not really even a mess, it's just a little uncomfortable right now but it'll pass. Don't all things...pass?"

"Yeah, like infectious diseases." Cam snatched up the book he'd just put down, thrusting it under Mandy's nose. "Read this." Mandy batted the book away. "I'm serious. There's more how-to in romance than in anything you could find on the self help shelf: real problems solved by real people."

"Real people named Octavio and Francesca?" Mandy snatched the book and stared at the couple on the cover, locked in a wild embrace. "*Forever, My Love*?"

Cam nodded. "The second book in the triangle trilogy I told you about."

"So they didn't solve the problem in book one?" Mandy chided. "Sound like great role models."

"I'm serious. You're in the same jam Octavio and Francesca—see, you remembered their names—are in their love story triangle."

"I'm not going to read this to figure out what I should do about Boston, Cam. That's not happening."

Cam's eyes widened at something over her shoulder and Mandy whipped around. Boston stood six feet away at a chair. When his eyes met hers, he studied her for a moment, no smile, no nod of acknowledgement. Mandy's heart tumbled to her stomach. Without responding, she turned around.

"Are you going to do anything?" Cam whispered. He smiled and nodded at Boston in a false greeting, then leaned closer to Mandy. "I can go pound him for you."

"No, don't do that—"

"He's coming over. Want me to stay and smash in his teeth or go get a refill?"

Mandy didn't have time to answer, Boston was already there at her side, his scent oozing over her senses, soaking into every vulnerable nerve inside of her. She looked up into his face and her pride drowned.

Cam rose, crossed his arms over his chest and tilted his head at Boston. "Hey."

"Hey." Boston extended his hand for a shake. "Cam, right?"

Taken aback, Cam fidgeted before shaking hands. "Yeah. I'm going to go get a refill. Want anything, Mand?"

Mandy's stomach was too knotted to put anything in it. She nodded, and watched Cam walk away, not sure what to expect from Boston.

"Mind if I sit?" he asked.

The initial jittering she felt when she first saw him was vanishing, in its place her bruised ego and shredded pride were resurrecting themselves. She sat up straight, absently clutching the book Cam had given her to her chest. "Fine."

Boston sat his dark eyes intense and tight on hers. "I thought I might find you here."

"You—you came to see me?"

"Yeah, and because this place is the only place where I can fully get my head out of my butt."

"How nice for you."

"Look, I just don't want it to be awkward between us now."

What did he expect? Mandy shifted, anger and frustration bubbled beneath her skin. "Why should it be awkward?"

His eyes narrowed. "I don't know, but I don't want it to be."

"It's not," Mandy lied. "So that's it?"

The corner of his jaw knotted. "What else is there?"

"We kissed. I don't know about you but that usually means something."

"It does when it isn't a ploy. I don't want to make it something that it's not. I wouldn't do that to you. You deserve..." He stopped, his intense gaze seeping deeper into her core, softening what was left of her hard heart.

"What do I deserve?" When he didn't answer but merely shook his head, Mandy's pride took a direct slug. He let out a sigh, looked down at the pile of books between them, hers and Cam's now in a mixed up mess. Even though he'd told her that he didn't have feelings for his ex, that didn't mean he had feelings for her, and Mandy took the revelation like an arrow through her soul.

She took a deep, strengthening breath. "It's no biggie." She watched his eyes for any change, to see if the comment hurt him in the slightest, but didn't see anything except the same intensity he'd come to her with.

His gaze fell to the pile of books. He picked one up and a grin crept on his lips. "Those are Cam's."

"Yeah?" His eyes lit. "I had a roommate that swore by romances."

"Yeah?"

He nodded. "Said they were pretty good reading."

"Seriously?" A light laugh fluttered from Mandy's

chest. She glanced around for Cam, wishing he was back defending his pile of fluff. "I haven't read one since junior high school."

Boston's eyes latched on the romance book she held at her chest. "Oh, this is one of Cam's too. He was recommending it to me." When his expression turned to teasing, she felt better, like things between them were going to be okay, even if the two of them weren't going to be anything more than just friends. She reminded herself that he was healing, and that she had to be okay with that. "Tell you what, I'll read one if you read one."

Boston shuddered and she let out a laugh. "No thanks," he said. He stood and stuck his hands in his front pockets.

"Scared you might learn something?" Mandy raised a brow.

He laughed and the warm sound trickled down to her toes. A pang of sorrow echoed through her, wishing things could be different. When his laugh died and he simply stared into her eyes, she held her breath. He was so beautiful.

Cam came back with a drink, his brows furrowed over suspicious eyes. "So."

"So." Boston rocked back on his heels.

Mandy's hands fisted and her insides tensed with frustration at Cam's lousy timing. She needed to talk more with Boston.

Cam handed her the drink. "There you go, gorgeous."

Confusion, then what looked like intrigue covered Boston's face for a moment. "I'll let you two get back to your reading," Boston said. "See you tomorrow, Mandy."

"Yeah, see ya."

After he'd left, Mandy felt a hollowing inside. She gazed blankly at the book in her arms.

"What did he say?" Cam situated himself on the couch, readying for his next read and picked up *Hot Fun in the Summertime*.

Mandy let out a sigh. "He doesn't read romances." She sat back and resisted the urge to stare at Boston over her shoulder. Instead, she tossed the book in her hands back into the pile.

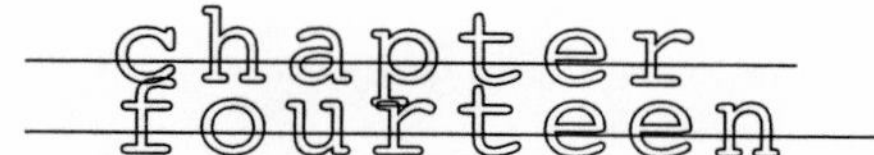

chapter fourteen

This was the first day of work that Mandy dreaded, and she didn't like it. She didn't want anything or anyone to get in the way of her job enjoyment. To top off her mood, the usually blue summer sky was filling with brooding clouds. On the drive to the main office, she stared out the window, nibbling on her acrylic thumb nail. Her white tips had taken a beating. She needed to get in for another manicure soon.

Marc kept glancing over, and his suspicion made her stomach uneasy. "So, you going to tell me what that kiss was all about yesterday?"

"All I'll say is that it wasn't really a kiss. It was an act for that chick that showed up. That's why I said Boston is still clean."

"Didn't look like no show to me."

"Shut up, Marc."

"Hey, if he was using you, I'll fire his butt from the job. And who freaking cares about the bet. That's just—"

"We were both using each other," Mandy snapped, sending a sharp silence into the air. "He was trying to make her jealous."

"Man. You coulda fooled me."

"You're easy to fool, fool," Mandy chided with a light shove at his arm. She wanted to end the discussion.

He pulled the car into the parking lot and Mandy saw the guys waiting, coffee cups in hand. A shiver of anticipation raced down her spine. Both A.J. and Boston were intently watching her.

Mandy scooted closer to Marc so one of the guys could sit next to her, though her insides trembled at the possibility that it would be Boston.

The truck swayed as the men climbed over the back, then the door opened and A.J. peered in, steaming cup just under his lips. His eyes twinkled in a grin. "Morning." He slid in next to her. The scent of his coffee mulled with the scent of him, a scent that took Mandy back to the night of their date, to when he'd surrounded her, held her and kissed her.

He shut the door and Marc backed the truck out of the parking lot. Only a thread of disappointment dangled inside of Mandy. It was hard to think of anything but A.J. with his arm and thigh brushing into her side.

"How are you this morning, baby doll?" A.J. sipped from his cup and for some reason the sound poured warmth right through Mandy to her toes. She couldn't help but look at his mouth. His lips pulled back into a grin.

She lifted her gaze to his. "I'm fine, A.J. How are you?"

"Doing well, thank you."

Marc snorted. Mandy shoved her elbow into his ribs. "Hey!"

"What did you do last night?" Mandy asked, partly curious, partly wanting to cover up the silence. She reached over and turned on the CD player. Someone rapped from the speakers.

"I was out with a friend." Once again his deep sip

stirred something inside of her and she forced herself to stare at the long stretch of road ahead of them. The news surprised her and, even more shocking was the pang of jealousy.

"Oh. Cool." She wondered who the woman was, where they'd gone, what they'd done. Had he kissed her?

When he took another sip from his coffee her eyes were drawn to his mouth again, and her mind flashed pictures of him in a tight embrace with some faceless woman. His grin seemed to say that he enjoyed that she was staring at his mouth. His eyes did their own lazy scan of her lips then, and her heart fluttered.

"And how about you?" His voice was low and raspy.

"Uh, my night was good, thanks. I went to the bookstore."

Marc let out another snort. Mandy ignored him, facing A.J. "I met a friend there." Why did she feel compelled to tell him that? She held his gaze, and thought she saw his eyes narrow slightly.

He lowered his cup, holding it in both hands at his lap. "He was a lucky man then."

Marc let out a chuckle and Mandy sent her elbow back, making sure she got him in the ribs. His laugh stopped with a cough.

"He's also gay," Marc tossed.

"Cam is not gay."

"Coulda fooled me."

"Guys just *think* he's gay. Believe me, he most definitely is not gay."

A.J.'s right brow arched. A smile of intrigue curved his lips. "You sound like a woman who knows."

"And I do," Mandy piped.

Marc shot her a look twisted with irony. "Are we talking about the same guy? The guy who reads romance novels because he can't get a girl?"

"This conversation is now over." Mandy crossed her arms over her chest. She stared straight ahead, Marc's teasing laugh grating on her pride like nails on glass. To her right, A.J. didn't react except to take another long sip of coffee.

They arrived at the site a few minutes later and everyone piled out. It was the first time Mandy had a chance to gauge Boston. He nodded cordially her direction as he slipped on his tool belt.

A.J. yanked his red bandana out of his back pocket and tied it around his head, his Caribbean-green gaze on Mandy. The air between her, A.J. and Boston seemed a little lighter today and Mandy was glad.

Marc and Larry headed off, leaving Boston on her right and A.J. on her left.

"Where's your bathing suit?" A.J. asked.

Mandy glanced down at her denim shorts and red tee shirt. "Giving my skin a break today."

Boston cleared his throat and Mandy looked at him. Something she couldn't read darkened his eyes, aimed at A.J. He crossed his arms over his chest. "Quit looking at her like she's your next meal."

A low chuckle rumbled out of A.J.'s chest. The muscles in his arms shifted as he knotted the bandana at the back of his head. He took a step in Boston's direction, bringing their noses within inches. "It's none of your business what I choose to look at." He held Boston's gaze for a long breath that Mandy held in her chest, then he turned on his heel and with a whistle, headed into the house.

Boston stared after him, his jaw tense as stone. Then his hard stare slid to her.

"What are you getting all riled up about?" she snapped, irritated that he was defending her. She didn't belong to him.

His brown eyes shot wide. "He's salivating over you."

"Yeah? So what?" Mandy started toward the house, pleased that Boston seemed shocked, struggled even with her reaction. "He knows what he wants."

"Yeah, like a lion wants a gazelle." His shoulder brushed hers as he kept pace. "You don't care that he sees you like that?"

Mandy stopped, sending fine dirt in cloudy billows around them. "He sees me as desirable—irresistible—I believe was his exact word. I love it!" She started into the house but felt the steely grip of Boston's hand wrap around her arm and hold her back. Heart pounding in her chest, she stood face-to-face with him.

Emotions passed over his face she tried to read: disappointment, surprise, hurt, anger. Could he really care enough to have a kaleidoscope of feelings for her? The scent of his laundry detergent and his skin swam into her senses and plunked down next to her common sense, nearly suffocating her resolve. "Why do you care, anyway?" she asked.

"I've seen guys like that operate, that's all." He kept his voice low, his body near as if he knew his heat could melt her on the spot. She thrust her chin up. "I don't want to see you get used or worse," he said.

"I've already been used," Mandy hissed out. His

angry expression shifted to hurt. She opened her mouth to take the words back but her voice stalled. Overhead, the thickening clouds blocked the sun and sent dark shadows over his face.

He released her arm with a look of resolve. "I thought we'd settled that. Obviously only one of us did."

Mandy swallowed a hard lump. "We had. I did. That was stupid of me to bring it up."

"No." He shook his head. "You're right. You have every right to hang on to that."

But she hated people that hung on to grievances and didn't forgive. Clearly he was the kind of man that did not hang on—and he'd expected her not to either. He went alone into the house. Mandy waited a moment to join him, sure she'd just made the stupidest mistake of her life.

Rumbling overhead, feisty clouds twisted together in billows of grey and black. Even without a single drop of rain the air was starting to smell damp. Jagged bolts of electric white lightening stabbed the earth in the distance. Mandy shot nails into the wood, her eyes scanning the horizon, the wide expanses of dirt dotted with new construction, and wondered how much longer the work day would last.

It had been fairly quiet with the exception of Larry's portable CD player and Marc and Larry's never-ending woman chatter. Larry was still with Samantha—a record—and he was happy to be monogamous. Mandy caught enough of their conversation to hear where Larry's life was. But the string tight quiet tying her, Boston, and A.J. left her feeling like she was working on a bed of nails.

A.J. had whistled some but hadn't said much during the morning. She missed his playful teasing. Boston hadn't said a word. Mandy let out a sigh and shot off another nail. *Man, if this is triangles, send me to Bermuda and into a dark hole—anywhere but here. I'd much rather have friendships than the whole relationship thing,* she thought, glancing at Boston. His back was to her as he hammered a few feet away. Today he wore faded black denim shorts. Half-circles of perspiration shown under the armpits of the gray tee shirt he had on.

There were so many other things she could have said to him. She couldn't make what she'd said go away, either. All she could hear over and over in her brain was, *I've already been used.*

She closed her eyes and leaned her forehead against the closest two-by-four. She hadn't meant to hurt his feelings, to demolish whatever fragile thoughts he'd maybe had of her. One thoughtless sentence...

A hand on her shoulder brought her eyes open. A.J. stood near, his twinkling eyes concerned. "You okay?"

Mandy nodded and took a deep breath. She fought the urge to look over A.J.'s shoulder to gauge Boston's reaction but couldn't. Her gaze shifted and there he was, pausing from his work, watching.

Mandy's heart pounded just looking at him. The pain she felt for her snide remark once again tore through her. Another rumbling from the arguing clouds above filled the airspace. She looked at A.J., studying her intensely. "I'm okay, thanks."

His hand was strong and sure on her shoulder. He

gave her light squeeze, then he took in a deep breath and looked out over the horizon. "Looks like we won't be working much longer if this storm doesn't pass."

"Marc'll be ticked," Mandy murmured, following A.J.'s gaze.

"It'll throw us back a little but not much. We're almost finished here." A.J.'s gaze scanned the nearly completed second story of the house. Then his eyes found hers. "And we'll be done."

Mandy took a deep breath. The idea of the job being over caught her off guard and she didn't like the sadness creeping over her. Her brother hired his crews according to the job, and she knew they had more houses to frame over the summer. Whether or not any of these guys would be part of the team she was assigned to was a guess. If the three of them couldn't work civilly together, Marc might place her somewhere else.

A.J. reached up and skimmed the side of her face with his rough fingers. He moved closer and for a second Mandy had the fleeting picture that he would kiss her. But her fantasy of being pressed against the wood and kissed good and hard did not star A.J, as much as she cared for him.

"You're a hard worker."

"Thanks, A.J. I like to think I carry my load."

His fingers were still on her cheek, wandering now, lingering near her chin. "Oh, you carry your load. And you make coming to work everyday a pleasure." He held her chin poised and eyed her mouth with a look that sent warmth over Mandy's body.

A furious crackle in the clouds broke the silence but not the intense way he was staring at her lips—with a look that caused Mandy to take an involuntary step back, bringing her spine against the framed wall. She wet her lips with a nervous swipe of her tongue. A.J.'s thumb gently brushed her chin, skimming her lower lip.

From the thundering clouds, a light, misty rain began to fall.

The thundering pound that followed was not from the heavens, but from Boston who stormed over, ripping both Mandy and A.J.'s gazes to him. His tanned skin pulled taut over the rigid angles of his face.

"Why are you letting him do this?" he demanded, glaring at Mandy.

"Excuse me?"

"He's touching you."

"Yeah? So what. I like it."

"He's playing with you."

A.J.'s hand slipped down to his side and he shifted feet, as if itchy inside. The jagged current bouncing between them electrified the air, and with the rain coming down now in light bullets that hit the protective wood sheathing, voices raised a notch.

"He's not playing with anyone. He's a man. He wouldn't do that."

Boston let out a snort. "That's exactly why he would do it, Mandy. You're just too naive to see it."

Mandy's mouth opened. "I am not naïve. I happen to know exactly what's going on between A.J. and me. I'm not clueless here."

Boston crossed his arms. "What is going on between you?"

"I don't think that's any business of yours." A.J.'s calm voice seemed to only annoy Boston further. His fiery glare slid over.

"I've seen you operate, man." Boston tapped A.J. on the chest. "You're smoother than a car salesman and about as sincere."

"Control your fuse." A.J.'s hands fisted. "I think you'd better stop while you're still in one piece."

Boston's arms tensed at his sides and Mandy stepped between them. "Okay, this is over now. We're all friends here, we work together. Let's be professional about this."

"This isn't about work, baby doll."

"Like hell it isn't." Boston took a step in A.J.'s direction and Mandy pressed her hand to his chest to hold him back. "You come here every day with your mouth drooling and lay your trap like some shifty fox."

A.J.'s body twitched. Mandy thought he looked ready to combust and her heart sped in her chest. A half-smile twisted his lips, he shook his head. "See, you're too young to control yourself, to know when to back off."

"I'll back off when you stop messing around with her. She's not like you. Anybody with half a brain can see that. What makes you think she'd go for a freeloader, anyway?"

A.J.'s eyes slit. Mandy held her breath. When A.J. stepped forward she slapped her palm on his chest to stop him. "A.J., don't."

"What's going on here?" Marc's demand sliced through the sound of pelting rain as he strode over.

Neither Boston nor A.J. said anything for a long, steamy moment. Mandy's left hand stayed fastened on A.J.'s hard chest, her right on Boston's. She looked at Marc and stumbled on words. "We're…we just—"

"Having a friendly little chat," A.J. answered Marc but his gaze stayed locked on Boston.

"There's nothing friendly about it," Boston ground out.

"Okay, okay." Marc's gaze flicked from A.J. to Boston. "One of you needs to go take a leak or get a drink or something. *Now*."

Boston jerked back and stormed across the floor to the stairs.

Marc set his hands on his hips and let out a sigh. Overhead, thunder rumbled as the clouds rolled over the site, dropping sheets of water outside the protection of the house. "I'm not even gonna ask what that was all about. I don't want it happening again. I don't need drama. Get back to work."

"Yes, sir, boss," A.J. nodded.

Marc's impatient stare held Mandy for a moment before he stomped back to Larry who merely shot a casual glance the way of the disturbance, and didn't even stop working.

A look of wary curiosity was on A.J.'s face now. Her hand was still on his chest and she drew it back, the awkward moment quiet.

"What do you make of all this, baby doll? Ever been the subject of a man's fight?"

Mandy drew her lower lip between her teeth. "No. Can't say it's all I thought it'd be, either," she murmured, glancing over where Boston had disappeared.

A.J. scrubbed his jaw, took in a deep breath, and followed her gaze. "Yeah, well, there's no cameras here. No script."

Mandy shivered from the awkward moment.

As usual, A.J. seemed to read her thoughts. The idea comforted but disconcerted her at the same time.

"What *are* you doing with me, A.J.?"

He seemed taken aback, and for a moment his green eyes averted. "I'm not playing with you, if that's what you're worried about." His intense gaze held her still. "Mandy, from day one I thought you were something else. Sweet." He reached out and stroked the side of her face with his wet finger. "Innocent." But the look in his eye was not the look she had seen there before, this look had sadness in it. Regret. Then he looked over her shoulder at where Boston had gone.

Mandy wasn't sure, but something inside of her wound tight around her heart, like the moment between her and A.J. had changed everything. A door had closed.

Mandy took a deep breath, then wrapped her arms around herself to combat another shiver. More than anything she wanted to find Boston and talk to him, but she'd never put out two fires at once before.

A.J. nodded his head in the direction of the stairs. "Go talk to him."

"Can we get back to work, please?" Marc hollered from across the floor.

Again A.J. gestured with his head for her to go. "Go."

"I need to get a drink," Mandy called to Marc.

Marc rolled his eyes, threw up his hands like a ref after a foul and then waved an arm in the direction of the stairs.

She found Boston. He stood in the front door casing, both hands gripping the frame as he looked out. Mandy crossed to him slowly, her mind racing with what to do, what to say. His grey tee shirt clung to the muscles of his back and arms. The rain was thoroughly drenching his hair, his head looked like he wore a glistening cap. The tips of his waves turned up and framed his face like a halo.

He looked over and the dark intensity in his eyes made her insides swarm with uncertainty.

Another scream of thunder wracked the air around them. The building felt as though it shook, but Mandy was sure it was just her body trembling. Outside the structure, rain pelted the dirt in a million splats.

"I don't know what to say." She approached with caution, stopping a good six feet away from him.

Along his arms, muscles shifted and tensed as he held onto the door frame. He didn't respond, just stared at her, and the jumble of feelings coursing through her was thrilling, frightening and wondrous.

"Do you think I led A.J. on?"

"Maybe."

"I was just being friendly."

"You were flirting."

Mandy's eyes popped. "So what if I was. I don't belong to anybody. I have the right to—"

"Not on the job, Mandy. It's not professional."

Mandy was mortified that he'd seen her attempts at friendship as unabashed flirting when she'd been trying to protect him, and preserve her heart.

"Maybe you're just peeved because I wasn't flirting with you."

"You were flirting with me too, that's the problem."

Aghast, Mandy stepped back, robbed of speech. A

flush heated her from head to toe. "I was trying to protect you."

"From what?" He let out a frustrated sneer.

"From…I don't know. Females in general."

"Yeah, right. You were flirting. Blatantly flirting when you knew I was trying to stay away from women. You made it impossible."

Mandy's mouth fell open. Shock made her blink at him. She couldn't defend herself because part of what he said was true. She just thought nobody knew what was inside her heart but her.

She took another step back. She wanted to run somewhere—anywhere—and get away from him and this horrible moment.

Boston stormed from the door and in two long strides was against her. His hands, warm and firm, cupped her cheeks and the next thing she knew, his damp lips were on hers. Fire shot from her head to her shaking knees.

Just as fast as he'd grabbed her, he released her, and stood back, dark eyes locked with hers, a fast pant in his chest.

Mandy's mind was blank. Her heart pounded against her ribs, in her ears, pulsing flames to her cheeks. A few feet away, Boston's erratic breath started to slow. He took another step backward, his gaze still fastened to hers.

Mandy's blood thudded with uncertainty. Boston shot one last hard look at her before starting toward the stairs. Taking in a deep breath, Mandy waited until he had vanished before she pressed her fingers to her lips and closed her eyes.

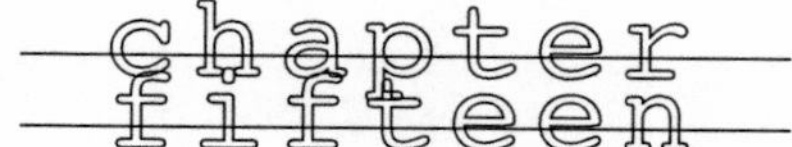

Nothing cleared her head like the scent of bookstore. Mandy stood just inside the glass doors of Barnes and Noble and breathed deep. She even smiled, though her insides were still a mess after what had happened earlier at the site.

That kiss.

She touched her lips again. Through her body a current both sweet and curious buzzed as she recalled the way Boston's hands had held her face, as his lips had taken hers.

Why had he kissed her? He'd been angry, accusing her of flirting with him, tearing open her private dreams, embarrassing her. Of course he didn't know her private dreams included him, but he'd gotten so close she wondered if males were smarter than females gave them credit for in things romantic.

Dazed thinking about the kiss, she wandered into the store with a small grin on her lips. Cam was supposed to meet her and she headed for the back of the building to the lounge area but didn't see him or his black backpack.

She decided to search the romance section. The first aisle was empty so she rounded the corner to the second. It, too, was empty. Curiosity had her slowing, eyeing the shelves and wondering if even she might learn something from reading a romance. She glanced around, and, finding herself alone, studied the titles. *Impossible Man. Love In the Afternoon. Heart's Desire.* She wondered if you actually got what you picked up or if romance titles were creatively ambiguous like titles were in other genres. *Temptation Street. Marked for Love. Blinded, Bound and Beautiful.*

Mandy rolled her eyes.

Somehow she doubted the answers to her problems would be found in the pages of a romance novel, or in any book for that matter. She'd never run away from issues, always faced them head on. Boston's kiss had swiped the embarrassment she'd felt at his accusations and when he'd walked away, she'd been helpless to go after him and pound him.

She checked the last aisle, found it empty and headed to the home improvement section in search of house plans.

At the end of a corner, she bumped into A.J.

"Well, how goes it, baby doll?" His green eyes glittered. He smelled like he'd just emerged from a shower, clean and soapy. Khaki shorts showed off his enviable tanned legs and his silky, flowered shirt made him look like he was ready to party.

"I'm good, A.J. You? What're you doing here?"

"Looking for you." With a teasing smile he glanced around. "And books."

"Me?" She shifted feet, grinned.

He reached out and skimmed her nose with his finger. "Yeah. You didn't think I read, did you?"

The contact caused her heart to skip a beat with

uncertainty. She shrugged. "You're a college graduate and an accountant. I assume you've done your share of studying."

His cheery demeanor shifted slightly. Mandy wondered if she'd said the right thing. The last thing she'd ever do is hurt A.J.

"Can I get you a drink?" he asked.

Mandy was glad to be off the topic. She nodded. He held out his elbow to her and for a moment she stared at it. Then she slipped her hand around it and let him lead her into the café.

"You looking for a particular book?" he asked.

"No, just looking. Actually, I'm meeting a friend here." She watched his reaction. His smile only deepened.

"Why is he keeping you waiting?"

Mandy looked around the café, but she knew she wouldn't see Cam there. He hated getting their drinks because the guy behind the counter flirted with him, so he insisted she get their orders. He was probably running late at Five Buck.

They stopped at the counter and the waiter that liked Cam, dressed in black jeans and a black tee greeted them. He reached up and smoothed his black, dew-drop hair and smiled, his gaze lingering on A.J.

"I'll have an Italian soda. Make it caramel and vanilla with cream," Mandy said.

The young man nodded, then his bored look shifted with interest to A.J. "You, sir?"

Oblivious to the thorough scan he was getting from the waiter, A.J. studied the menu through squinting eyes. "I'll have a mint freeze."

"My favorite." The waiter leaned forward with a twist on his lips. "You won't be disappointed. Promise."

A.J. seemed to finally get the underlying pleasure of the waiter's comment because his face went flat. Mandy almost laughed.

He looked at Mandy. "You didn't answer my question." He seemed to relax just turning his attention to her.

"He's probably delayed."

"But he keeps his girlfriend waiting?" A.J. leaned against the glass display case that held cakes, cookies, and brownies.

"He's not my boyfriend. He's just a friend."

The blender whirred loudly and Mandy looked over. The waiter was staring at A.J. and her face quirked into another grin before she returned her gaze to A.J. The look on A.J.'s face puzzled her, as if he was saying, 'is that so?' He didn't say anything, just pinned her with his smiling eyes.

The waiter handed them their drinks. Mandy started through the dozens of tables and chairs situated in the café. A.J. followed her.

"How about we sit?" A.J. suggested.

"I'd better look for my friend first," she tossed over her shoulder.

"Sure." A.J. stayed with her, now his shoulder brushed hers. His eyes twinkled. "Mind if I come along? I'd like to meet one of your friends."

"Sure. Okay."

They walked back to the lounge area and it was still empty. Mandy let out a sigh, and sipped her drink. A.J.'s arm brushed hers. He stood so close, Mandy wondered why when she'd been certain that she'd seen some kind of closure in his expression at work earlier. He seemed like the same A.J. she'd been working with the last few weeks: teasing, flirty and glad to be around her. Maybe that didn't mean anything. Maybe that's how real men handled it—getting over and on with life—when relationships didn't work in their favor.

"He not here?" A.J. looked around.

"I don't see him."

"How about we steal this couch?" A.J. crossed to the same couch Mandy had sat on with Boston that first day she'd run into him here.

"Sure."

After settling into the cushions, he smiled up at her. "You go get the books you want. I'll wait here until you come back, just in case there's a rush." With a laugh he glanced around at the nearly empty reading area.

"Okay. Thanks." Mandy set off in the direction of the home improvement section, sipping her drink and pondering running into A.J. Not that the coincidence bugged her. She was glad that he liked to read. In her mind, reading was number five in the four food groups: brain food.

After perusing the selection before her, she chose some of her favorites: *Bungalows of the Early Thirties*, *American Greek Revival* and the *Architecture of Frank Lloyd Wright* plus a new release, *New York Skyscrapers*.

A.J. had his smiling gaze on her the instant she emerged from the depths of the shelving, and her insides did a soft somersault. He had an affect on her, she couldn't deny that. It annoyed her that she couldn't put aside her feelings for him completely. Her heart, she guessed, was not wholly parked in Boston's camp, not sure how he really felt about her.

But he'd kissed her.

She smiled.

"What are you smiling about?" A.J. asked as she sat down, her books sliding off her lap onto the cushions between them.

"I found a new book." No way would she tell A.J. that Boston had kissed her. She held up the *New York Skyscrapers* volume. "Cool, huh?"

He nodded and stood. "Guess it's my turn. Be right back." Drink in hand, he left.

Mandy opened the new book, but she couldn't concentrate. Her whole body was taken in the memory of Boston striding over all intense and...The thought caused her to blink and shake her head. He couldn't possibly be jealous. Could he?

She looked around the store, wishing he was there, wishing she could ask him why he'd kissed her. That kiss had meant something, and she couldn't think of any thing else until she knew what.

Cam might shed some light on the subject. Where was he? She reached into her bag and plucked out her cell phone, then checked for messages. There were none. She knew his employer was apt to keep him after work if a rush hit. If something else had come up, she was sure he'd call.

A.J. came back, his blue eyes on her as he sat back down. He had such teasing eyes, and an inviting appeal that lingered in the air around him, heady and alluring as that enticing cologne he wore.

Mandy peered at his selection: the new *Esquire,* this

one with Angelina Jolie on the cover. Mandy didn't stare at the actress wearing only a long, white, man's shirt. For some reason, the image sent a pitch of jealousy straight to her stomach. She sat up straight and sipped, mortified when her deep slurp only rattled ice cubes.

A.J.'s eyes narrowed a little. "You don't like my selection?"

"It's okay," Mandy shrugged. How had he known what she was thinking? And why was jealousy still lodged in her gut? She shouldn't care what kind of women A.J. found attractive. "Is she why you bought the magazine?" she asked, curious.

He seemed pleased that she asked, and Mandy bristled inside thinking he could read her that easily.

"I like the magazine." His voice was silky and low, and slowly smoothed out Mandy's tight feelings. "She doesn't hold a candle to you, baby doll."

Mandy laughed. "Yeah, right." Inside she was a bluster of emotions as scattered as fallen leaves.

A.J. set the magazine aside and leaned over. His arm slid behind her on the couch. His other hand lifted, and his finger touched the tip of her nose. "You're..."

Mandy's heart flipped like a fish out of water. He was so close and so intently staring at her. She was afraid: afraid of how she felt, of what this meant, of what he would do.

"Today, you said you liked it when I touched you."

Mandy's throat drew into a knot she couldn't swallow. She couldn't speak, either. She just nodded.

"I like to touch you, baby doll," he whispered now, his face drawn tight, earnest. His finger slipped from her nose to her jaw and traveled slowly to her chin, then to her lower lip. Instinctively, her lips parted.

An ache, empty and wide, opened inside of her. His strong masculine aura swirled around her head, and her eyes closed as her mind fogged with the memory of the way he'd held her and kissed her on the porch. He'd made her feel so safe, so protected. His arms had taken every coherent thought and sent it into oblivion, leaving her feeling treasured. Before she could stop herself, she was leaning.

His finger tapped her lip and Mandy's eyes flew open. He was inches away, his green eyes locked with hers.

"Is this what you want?" His warm breath fanned her lips. She did. But she didn't. Only hours ago, Boston had stormed across the room, grabbed her face and laid a kiss on her mouth that Mandy so wanted to think meant something, claimed something: her.

But how could she know?

Yet here was A.J. Not the tornado that Boston was, a cyclone that if his path ever finally crossed hers she would be caught up in and submit to. No, with A.J. she felt like dessert.

She took a deep breath and eased back a few inches so she could take in more air, think, decide.

He didn't look at all surprised that she had moved away from him. In fact, the wary look on his face left Mandy glad that she'd decided against indulging in the kiss.

She held his gaze for a long time but didn't answer his question. The wariness he wore changed into the faintest disappointment before the unmistakable look of acceptance crept into his features. He picked up the magazine and his attention shifted to the open pages before him.

Forget Boston and his tornado. Beside her a typhoon simmered. A.J. looked his usual calm self, but around them energy whirred, the undercurrent of which kept Mandy from being able to concentrate on anything but A.J. sitting next to her, calculatedly turning one page at a time. Every time she snuck a peek to see if he was really reading, his eyes were never anywhere but on the page in front of him. But she didn't buy the act. It bugged her that he could read her and that he thought she couldn't read him. Was he playing a game? Did he really think she could sit so close to the storm and not see it?

She set her book aside and stared at him, waiting.

Instantly, she knew he sensed her for his movements slowed. The page he was so intently reading shook a little when he turned it. Then his green eyes lifted to hers. The intensity there made her stomach flip. She'd seen that look before and her insides trembled.

"I think you better confess," she said.

He tilted his head. The faintest smile played on his lips. "Confess? I haven't done anything."

"You're sitting there, pretending to read that magazine. *Pretending.* You've got something to say, why don't you just say it?"

He leaned forward, set the magazine aside without another thought and moved close enough to her that Mandy knew this part of their conversation he meant to keep between them.

His face became serious. "I'm angry, Mandy."

She was surprised that he'd so readily admitted what she'd suspected. Now, she wasn't sure what to brace for. "I sensed that."

"You're smart." His gaze skimmed every inch of her face. "It's another reason I can't give up on you, baby doll."

Mandy swallowed another knot of discomfort. "You…what do you mean, exactly?"

He reached out, took her hand, and held it between his two calloused palms. Lightly, he stroked the back side along the tendons of her fingers. "I mean that I want you."

Mandy looked away, his gaze so penetrating she was afraid he'd get her to admit that somewhere deep down she'd been unable to completely dismiss her feelings for him.

"Look at me, Mandy."

The comforting lure of his voice made her lift her eyes to his. "I thought a lot about it today, after work. It's all I could think about, in fact. I told you, I've never met anyone like you. I've never met anyone that has gotten to me like this. I think about you, Mandy, and it's not just at work. That's why I came tonight. I knew I'd find you here."

The honest urgency in his face caused Mandy's heart to thump. While she cared about him, was attracted to him, she wasn't sure theirs would be anything but a passing weather pattern. How could she lead him to think it would be anything more? Truth was, she doubted their priorities were the same. She wasn't sure her drive and determination boded well with his casual never-say-never attitude.

"Why do you want me, A.J?"

He seemed to take the moment to think about what

he was going to say. A heaviness drew the air around them into a closed place that made Mandy feel like they were alone in the store. When he didn't answer, she started feeling like she'd asked something too deep. "Maybe that was the wrong question."

"It was the right question." His hands tightened around hers. "You make me think I can have something I lost."

Regret darkened his usually smiling face. His jaw turned to stone. She wasn't sure what he'd lost, whether it had been a person he'd loved or a time he couldn't take back, but she wanted to know. If she could help him, regardless of what became of their friendship, she'd do it. "What did you lose?"

He let out a sigh and pulled his hand from hers. He pressed his fingertips together and pondered for a while. Out the corner of her eye, Mandy saw the kissing couple fondle their way over the LuvSac where they fell into kissing oblivion.

She turned her attention back to A.J. still gone somewhere in thought. "I made some stupid choices, took the easy path because I didn't think it would matter to anyone. It was my life, my decision. My family always thought I could do more with my life and wanted me to, but I didn't want…Nothing mattered that much for me to make the extra effort it took to work harder."

"But you work hard."

"Anybody can hammer in a nail, Mandy."

"Yeah, but you said you wanted to work outside with your hands. Isn't that good enough?"

"I don't know, is it?"

His eyes held hers in an unspoken question she could

never answer to his face. Mandy wouldn't be a weakling and look away, she held his gaze even though she saw the pain in his eyes when he seemed to read the truth.

"So even if I got a respectable job, it wouldn't be enough?"

Why did he have to lay his heart in front of her like this? Mandy's insides ached. "You have a respectable job. You're doing something you love."

He sat back on a harsh laugh. "I don't love construction, Mandy. It's easy. It's there. I don't close my eyes and get high on the scent like you do." He looked at her as if she stood a million miles out of reach.

"I...don't want to hurt you."

"Saying the words won't hurt me, baby doll." He sat back up, and with his finger, he reached out and trailed her cheek. "I can already see the answer in your eyes."

Mandy's gaze dropped to her hands, clasped on her lap. She could see why adults played games and danced around reality. Maybe hearts were better left on a cliff than thrown into an abyss where there wasn't even a surety that at the bottom of the chasm someone else would be there to catch it.

"Hey, there you are." Cam's chipper voice broke through the gulf of quiet resolution that seemed to be between them. A.J.'s hand quickly slipped from the side of her face to the couch.

Mandy turned and looked up at Cam, saw the wide-eyed look, and was sure her friend had caught the caress. "Sorry, didn't mean to interrupt," Cam coughed out.

For once, Mandy was relieved at Cam's timing. "Where were you?"

"Had to rush an order out to Saratoga Springs. Hey." Cam nodded in greeting at A.J.

A.J.'s face broke into the warm smile Mandy was used to. He stuck out his hand to Cam and they shook. "A.J."

Cam beamed. "Cam. Hey, I've heard a lot about you, man."

Oh no. Mandy cringed. The last thing A.J. needed was more confusion. He lifted a brow at Mandy but his tone remained cordial and he did not let on that he read anything more than a nice compliment into what Cam said. "Is that right? Mandy's a thoughtful woman."

"Woman." Cam's brows met for a moment. "Yes, she is. Well." He rocked back on his heels as if he finally sensed that something thick was in the air. "You gotten a drink yet, Mand?"

She held up her empty cup and rattled the straw. He nodded. "I'm going to go get something. You guys cool?"

"Yes, thanks, Cam."

He backed toward the café. "Nice to have met you, A.J."

"You too." A.J. nodded.

Once Cam had gone, A.J. looked at her, his green eyes on the verge of twinkling in that way that she loved. "Nice guy."

"Yeah, he is."

"I guess I'm surprised."

"You didn't think I had nice friends?" She laughed, glad the mood was lightening. She treasured their friendship and didn't want it to ever change, if that was possible.

"I knew you had nice friends, baby doll. I thought you were meeting Charlie here."

Mandy swallowed. "Oh. Well. No."

A.J. blinked slow and heavy, eyeing her. She wondered why he was easy to read sometimes and hard to read other times, like now. She so wanted to know what made him look like that—as if he'd just eaten a big gourmet meal but was still hungry.

Suddenly he leaned toward her and kissed her cheek. He snatched his magazine, stood, and tapped the Esquire against his palm. His eyes glittered in that familiar way that made Mandy's heart trip. "Charlie's a fool if he doesn't think you're irresistible. Goodnight, baby doll."

Mandy fell back against the couch like a balloon with a puncture. She blew out a breath, closed her eyes, and tried to sort one heart between two men. But her heart was not some field flower and she couldn't choose one man over the other based on which petal was left.

"Where'd A.J. go?"

She opened her eyes. Cam stood in front of her, minus a drink. "He left."

"He seems cool. You should go for him, Mand." Cam sat down, slid his backpack off.

"He is cool. He's super nice, thoughtful, gentlemanly."

"Not to mention totally into you. I saw him touching you." Cam unzipped his backpack but shot wiggling brows her direction.

"You saw? I was afraid of that."

"There's nothing wrong with it. It was awesome in fact. Like a scene from one of my books, the way he was looking like he could kiss you no holds barred. Sizzled."

Heat rose to Mandy's face. "Stop it."

"You're going to sit there and tell me you didn't like it?"

"No."

"Good, cause if you did I'd call you a liar. You were

begging for it."

"I wasn't begging for anything."

"You were practically in his lap!" Cam pulled out a paperback, opened it.

"Okay, maybe I was leaning."

"You were definitely leaning."

"Maybe I wanted it. But we didn't kiss, *as you saw*."

"Yeah, I was going to ask you why that didn't happen? I was, like," Cam let out a dog-like pant and grinned.

"He asked me if I wanted it and…I did, but I didn't."

"Still thinking about Boston?"

Mandy nodded. She stuck her thumb nail between her teeth. "He kissed me today."

"What?! Wait." Cam tossed his book aside and pulled his legs up on the couch in a cross-legged position. "Was this a real kiss or another one of his maneuvers?"

"This was real."

"Let me be the judge of that. Tell me what happened."

Mandy inched closer and lowered her voice. "We had a little thing *happen*, me, Boston and A.J."

Cam was salivating. "What kind of thing?"

"A little argument. Anyway, Boston got mad at A.J., accused him of luring me into a trap, and A.J. didn't like it. I seriously thought he would smash Boston's face in."

Cam's mouth dropped.

"So Boston goes downstairs to be alone and cool off and I followed him. One thing led to another and the next thing I knew, he was storming over, took my face in his hands and kissed me."

"Oh, man!"

Oh man was right. The memory sent Mandy's head into a spin as fresh as if Boston had just kissed her. She closed her eyes, smiling. "It was amazing."

"Then what?"

Mandy opened her eyes. "Then he walked away."

"He just left you there? After a kiss like that?"

Mandy nodded. "Can you see why I'm confused?"

"Freak yes." Cam fell back into the couch on a sigh. "Okay, obviously Boston laid claim there. I mean, you don't just kiss someone randomly like that unless you're Colin Farrell."

"You really think that's what it meant?"

"What else could it be? He was steaming jealous, Mand. That's obvious."

Mandy thrilled at the thought but couldn't accept it, the dream too unreal. "Unless he was just using me again."

Cam shot up to a sitting position. "If he was, I'm seriously coming to the site tomorrow and shooting a staple gun into that guy's brain."

Mandy blew out a sigh and Cam laid his hand over hers and patted. "Hey. I thought you two said you didn't like games and stuff?"

"We did. But—"

"Listen, I've read a lot about this. I know what I'm talking about. This is the classic climax for a triangle. Trust me. Boston is just getting warmed up."

"You think?"

Cam closed his eyes and nodded. "Trust me."

"What do I do about A.J.?"

"Hmm." Cam opened his eyes, took his hand from hers and rubbed his naked chin. "If only I could grow facial hair, I might look older. Girls might—"

"Cam, please."

"Right. Who do you like more?"

"That's the problem. I like them both for different reasons. A.J. is really confident. When I'm with him, I feel like…he just makes me feel like I'm the only woman in the world, and he *wants* me. He totally focuses on me. I feel safe. With Boston, it's more like I know that he cares, but he's tentative about where he puts his feelings. That appeals to me, especially with A.J. being more aggressive. Boston makes *me* want *him*. For the first time in my life, I can't make up my mind." Mandy fell back into the cushions on a groan. "Why is this happening to me?"

"Because you're a woman now, as A.J. so astutely put it. This is the big leagues. You're out there. Consider yourself lucky."

But having your heart torn in two was not glamorous, fun, or anything like the world portrayed it. It stunk knowing someone was going to get hurt, that she was going to do the hurting.

Mandy closed her eyes and tried to empty the stifling thoughts, but A.J.'s face meshed with Boston's and both were lodged in her brain.

"All this talk is making me thirsty," Cam said.

Mandy opened her eyes, remembered that he was without a drink. "I thought you went to the café?"

"That guy was working." Cam shuddered. "I didn't want to deal with it. Can you go get me something?" His face pleaded.

"Sure." Mandy waited while he dug out three dollars. He stuck the bills in her open palm and she stood. "I'll have a mint freeze."

"That's what A.J. had."

"Maybe it's a sign?" Cam's brows wiggled.

Mandy let out a snort. "It's the waiter's favorite."

"Ugh." Cam's eyes widened. "In that case, get me a Mochaccino Ice Storm."

The darkness and late hour surrounded Mandy like a foreboding tunnel as she drove home. Her trip to the bookstore had done nothing to ease the confusion she'd carried with her since Boston had kissed her, and had only gotten weightier after the visit with A.J.

At the moment, life stunk.

She tried listening to music, but that only made her edgier so she flicked off the CD player and left her mind open. *Whoever comes into my mind first, that will tell me where my heart is,* she decided, emptying her thoughts.

Boston.

Like a panther he crossed to her, cupped her cheeks, and took that kiss.

Mandy closed her eyes for a moment.

She opened them and searched for the comfort she expected to feel after the end of the little game, but what was in her mind now was A.J.'s face, his earnest eyes searching hers.

Mandy let out a groan and stuffed her free hand through her hair. She couldn't wait to get home, take a hot bath and sleep.

The familiarity of her street, of home in the distance soothed, giving a small lift to her mood.

Then she saw Boston's truck parked in front of her

house.

She almost stomped on the brakes but slowed instead. Her heart started to tap in her chest as she pulled up by his truck. She'd just said her goodbyes to A.J., and now here was Boston. She wasn't sure how her heart would respond. He looked over as she idled next to him. The expression on his face told her she'd startled him, but it vanished quickly.

Surely he wasn't sitting there, watching the house for her?

After she parked in the driveway, she took deep breaths trying to settle her fierce heart, but it was no use. The thrumming wouldn't stop.

She jingled her keys in her hand as she walked down the driveway. The warm summer night was silent with the exception of a chorus of crickets hiding in the bushes. Boston came her direction, his stride so confident the mere sight of his sleek walk caused her to break out in a sweat.

He stopped close, taunting her with his nearness. His brown eyes were fathomless in the darkness, staring like black fire into hers. Her whole body hummed. Why had she even doubted her feelings? Boston was the one she wanted, it was obvious to her now, and as plain as the beauty on his face.

Every thought of A.J. vanished.

Purposefully, Mandy waited for him to speak first. She doubted she could say a word anyway. Her heart was a hummingbird in her throat.

"Mandy, can we talk?" his voice was soft yet determined.

She nodded, turned, but stopped when his hand

wrapped around her bicep. "Out here."

"Okay. You want to sit?"

"I've been sitting out here since nine."

"I...I didn't know."

"I'm not blaming you. I just wanted you to know that I've been waiting because...." He looked away a moment. "Because I couldn't do anything else until I talked to you about today."

"Oh."

His sharp gaze pierced deep. "I kissed you."

A long silence followed. Mandy wasn't sure how to respond. Was he asking? Telling? Affirming? "Yes, you did."

"It wasn't like that kiss in Taco Bell."

"No, it wasn't."

He was struggling with this, she could tell by the way he shifted his feet. His hands didn't hang comfortably at his sides, he kept stuffing and unstuffing them into the front pockets of his khaki shorts.

She titled her head at him. "Tell me why you kissed me."

His eyes, wide and a little surprised, met hers. He swallowed. "I was...I'd had it. I was sick of A.J. coming on to you." He shoved his hands in his front pockets, then pulled them out again.

"Even if he was coming on to me—"

"He was coming onto you."

"It doesn't mean anything."

Boston shook his head. "I saw the way you looked at him."

Mandy's cheeks heated. "How did I look at him?"

"Like...I don't know, you were lit up."

"A very lame tendency I have."

"It's not lame. It's like A.J. says, it makes you irresistible." He thrust his hands back into his front pockets. "Jeez. Now I'm sounding like..."

"Finish that sentence, please." Mandy took a step in his direction, her chest filling with butterflies.

He stared at her long and deep. "I was jealous."

The admittance sent the butterflies in Mandy's chest to her fingers and toes.

"Does that surprise you?" he asked timidly. Thrill robbed Mandy of any words but didn't keep her from breaking out into laughter.

"You think this is funny?" His voice squeaked as he faced her again.

"No, I'm not laughing at you." Mandy waved her hand in front of her face as if that would help her stop laughing. "It's just that..." She took a deep breath "I am kind of surprised. I didn't think...you cared."

He stepped closer. The flecks of black in his eyes sparkled now, and his chest was rising in a fast rhythm that caught Mandy's heartbeat. "I didn't want you to care," she murmured.

"Why?"

"I saw how hurt you were and I knew you needed to be strong so your heart could heal."

He grinned and brought himself another step closer. The scent of his cologne had faded with the day but the smell caused Mandy to take a deep breath. "My heart healed the day I saw you glaring at me in Barnes and Noble." Tentatively he reached out and grazed the side of her face with his fingers. "You are...irresistible."

The smile Mandy had held back bloomed on her

face. "I like being irresistible."

"Yeah. It stinks for me, though."

Mandy's smile flatlined. "Why's that?"

"The bet's off."

"You cared about the bet?"

"Not really." He put his hands on her shoulders and held her steady. Mandy's body tingled. She drew her lower lip between her teeth.

"I want both of your lips," he said.

Mandy waited for the kiss with her heart banging. His brown eyes shifted to her mouth and the next thing she knew, his lips were against hers. She closed her eyes, and slipped her arms up around his neck.

Her body fused to his. Intoxicated by the elixir of a warm night and everything about him, she wanted to dissolve and lose herself, the heady feeling of his possessive arms wrapped tight around her causing joy to race through her and nearly burst from every pore.

His kisses grew light. He placed one on her upper lip, then he drew back, still holding her. "Mmm."

"You can kiss me any time."

"I'm glad to know that I have your permission."

Mandy lifted to her toes, slipped her arms up around his shoulders, and kissed him again. His arms wrapped around her. "I've wanted that since the first day."

"Since then?" he murmured against her hair.

"I can admit that I've had it for you since day one. I could tell you were the strong, silent type. And you were so brooding."

He eased back, a quirked look on his face. "*Brooding*?"

"And totally hot."

Boston's face twisted into wry amusement. "It still feels like I'm going to let you go and," one arm fell away from her and gestured, "you'll be swept off your feet by A.J."

A.J. was the furthest thing from her mind. "A.J.'s not sweeping me anywhere."

"The way he acts, sometimes I wonder. You guys went on a date, didn't you?"

"You *were* listening."

"I haven't missed a thing you've said, Mandy. Not a thing you've done."

Mandy laughed and eased back, relieved that she'd settled her heart. "Maybe we should go out. Do you date? Or do you just hang at the bookstore?"

"I date." He kissed her lips. "I'd like that, in fact."

"How about something *other* than the bookstore?"

"Or construction sites." He pressed his forehead to hers and let out a sigh. "You're the last thing I thought I'd find on the job."

The sunny day reflected Mandy's mood. As far as the eye could see, the sky was azure blue. White clouds drifted northward on their way to another place. Mandy was glad. No rain, today. The storms had passed.

In the warming air, she sensed another hot day and relished it. She'd dressed for heat, wearing her bathing suit and board shorts to maximize her tan. And she hoped Boston wouldn't be able to resist her either.

She tingled inside and nibbled on her nail as she stared out the window. One look at her faded nail tips and she pulled out her cell phone, and made an appointment for her next fill. She and Marc were driving to the home office to pick up the guys and she could hardly wait to see Boston. The fact that she'd come to peace with her troubled heart only made seeing him more thrilling.

It was then she noticed Marc's scowl.

"What's wrong?" she asked after she finished her call. She slipped her phone back in her pocket.

"Nothing." He scrubbed his face. He hadn't shaved, which, Mandy knew from experience, meant that he was in a social slump.

"What? No babes has left Jack a dull boy?"

He snorted. "More than dull. Dead. It's pretty lame when your kid sister dates with the regularity of a dog taking a dump, but—"

"What a sick analogy. That is precisely why you aren't having success, Marc. Your head is in the gutter."

"Is not."

"Is too."

"Oh, so you're going to sit there and tell me that you're attracted to A.J. and Boston because they're both intellects? Their bodies don't have anything to do with it?"

Mandy swallowed. "They're both attractive, I won't lie about that. But it's not what I focus on."

"Seems to work well for Larry."

"But that's Larry, Marc. You can be better than that. I think you're being too high school about this."

"Is that right?" Marc huffed, shooting her an incredulous look. "After one summer on the job, you're a pro at men?"

"I've snagged two, haven't I?"

"Jeez. Then it's true, isn't it. They both...jeez."

"It's not like that, Marc. It looks like that, but it's not."

"So the bet's off?"

Mandy couldn't keep the grin from her face. Marc sighed. "I only gave Boston two days, so I'm busted anyway. My guess is A.J. won the pot."

"Two days?" Mandy was aghast. "Boston is way stronger than that."

"I knew by that first kiss at Taco Bell he was a goner."

"I told you, that wasn't real."

"Oh, but since then you've had real? It's so unfair."

"What's unfair?"

"How easy it is for you to find someone."

"It hasn't been easy, Marc. It's one of the hardest things I've done, juggling two guys at once."

"You don't appreciate anything."

"Yes I do. I care about their feelings. I don't want to hurt either of them. Unlike you, I don't think relationships are disposable."

"Hey, I like disposable. Less complicated that way."

"Less complicated and less satisfying, that's why you are where you are."

Marc sighed. "You've always gotten what you wanted. And you always knew what you wanted, even when we were kids. Remember that time you told Dad you wanted a tool set for your birthday? A tool set for crying-out-loud. You were ten!"

Mandy's face flushed. Her friends had thought she was so strange when she gushed over the sparkling set of Allen wrenches, screwdrivers and hammers all set in a lovely black tool box. "Yeah."

"I wouldn't have wanted that. I'd have been too embarrassed."

"So when you go with Lar to these seedy places, do you really see what you want?"

Marc scratched his scruffy jaw. "I can appreciate a hot babe anywhere."

"What you're talking about is temporary, Marc. My guess is you're sick of that. You want something more now."

He looked over, grinned. "Just because you've succeeded in hooking two of my best guys doesn't mean you know anything."

Mandy shrugged but stood her ground. "It's the way I see it."

They pulled into the parking lot and saw the guys waiting around the back door of the office. "So who is it, Mand?" Marc maneuvered the truck into a parking place. "Which guy do you want?"

She looked out the window at Boston and smiled. Her heart took flight inside her body. Boston, she wanted Boston. Then her eyes shifted to A.J., standing next to him. A.J. sipped from a steaming cup, and watched her intently. Mandy bit her lip, her heart thrumming. When she hadn't been able to answer his question last night, she'd gotten the undeniable vibe that he had at last realized that her heart resided with Boston. She sent A.J. a small wave.

Marc raised his brow at her. The look sent an uncertain quivering through her system. "Ah, maybe she doesn't know who she wants after all."

"Boston," she shot. "Of course, it's Boston."

The guys were at the doors of the truck now, and

Marc still had an insipid smile on his face. Mandy wanted to slug him. She knew what she wanted. In her mind, only one heart fit perfectly next to hers.

The doors opened and Boston slid in next to her, the look in his eyes sparkling. "Hey," he said.

"Hey."

The truck wobbled as Larry and A.J. climbed over the back and settled into the bed. Marc started the engine and Mandy flicked on the CD. Suddenly, she couldn't think of anything to say.

She didn't know what to expect from work that day, but was relieved that A.J. was his usual cheerful self. Boston was attentive, smiling a secret smile at her as they worked. As a crew, they picked up where they'd left off: the final shears were being placed on the outside walls of the second floor.

With the inside framing in place, Mandy was able to get a real sense of the floor plan: rooms and halls were at last in order. Like her heart, she mused.

The guys worked from the outside on scaffolding and ladders as they secured the plywood outer walls. Marc refused to allow Mandy to climb up and do her part, citing that she could observe and learn just as easily by standing and watching, as opposed to risking her neck.

"He's right," Boston tossed over his shoulder. He made such a fine specimen of man perched up on that scaffolding, his golden-brown muscles glistening, flexing.

"Wouldn't want anything to happen to that pretty little head of yours, baby doll." A.J. turned and winked at her.

Mandy swallowed a knot. She so needed an ice

water. "Anybody want anything?" Were any of them parched like she was?

"You mean you're offering to do drudge work? What's gotten into you?" Marc laughed, then he rolled his eyes Boston's direction, making sure she saw his teasing expression.

Thankfully, Boston was busily engaged and missed Marc's obvious reference to her temporary insanity. "Since you won't let me up, I might as well make myself useful. I don't have a problem helping you guys out down here."

Boston looked over, a pleased grin on his face. "Thanks. I could use a water."

"No problem. Anybody else?"

"That works for me, too." A.J. said.

"Man, I wish I had a beer," Larry mumbled.

"Nothing like it to drown your sorrows," Marc said before shooting a stream of nails into the plywood.

Mandy shaded her eyes from the sun overhead. "What happened to Samantha?"

Larry shrugged, then whacked at a nail with his hammer.

"Don't tell me you got dumped." There was amusement in A.J.'s voice. "That a first for you?"

"It is, and I don't like it." Larry scratched his backside. "It stinks."

"But, hey," Mandy chirped, "look how long it lasted. I'm proud of you, Lar. You did good."

Over his shoulder, Larry shot her a twisted look that told her he could care less what she thought. "Whatever. It stinks. It ain't happening again."

Mandy laughed as she crossed to the water cooler.

She plucked three frosty water bottles from the ice and headed back to the conversation. "There's an old saying," she began. She stood under the scaffolding and looked up at Larry. "What goes around comes around."

"I feel the need to hock a loogie." Larry cleared his throat and aimed right at Mandy who ducked away, laughing.

"Better keep your philosophical commentary to yourself," Marc told her, jumping down. He strode over and took a bottle. "Larry's a bear when he doesn't have a woman."

"Well then, you two really are made for each other." Mandy handed A.J. a water now that he was there, waiting.

"Thanks, baby doll."

"You're welcome." Mandy was glad that he still used the term of endearment, glad that they could still be friends.

Boston climbed down and came to where they stood, all of them looking up at the side of the house nearly complete. He reached out and Mandy handed him a bottle. His smile melted her already soft insides.

"Guess I should see who won my pot," he said.

Marc whipped a wide-eyed look at Boston, then Mandy. "I should have known."

"Man, I'm the winner!" Larry lifted his water bottle skyward. "Something worked today. Yes." He chugged.

Why was it hard to look A.J. in the eye? Mandy tentatively met his knowing green eyes. A small smile lifted his lips. Then his gaze shifted to Boston. "I lost for sure," he said, his expression a mix of pleasure and something else—disappointment—Mandy thought.

"How long did you give Boston?" Mandy asked.

"Under your spell?" A.J. touched the tip of her nose lightly. "About a week."

"I won." Larry stuck both fists in the air. "I gave the guy two months." He crossed to Boston and playfully slugged his bicep with his water bottle. "Thought you'd never cave, man. Who was she?"

The guys exchanged glances. No one said anything, so Larry remained clueless. Mandy hid a blush by facing the house and gesturing the nearly finished project with a sweep of her hand. "The house is looking good."

"Looks great," A.J commented.

Marc wiped his mouth with the back of his hand and nodded. "Yeah."

"It's a nice floor plan." Mandy took a swig of the refreshing water. "I like it. Should be easy for Dad to sell. It's not too big for a starter house and nice enough for a small family."

"How about a single guy?" A.J. asked, his twinkling eyes meeting hers.

Suddenly, it was quiet and all attention turned to A.J. But he was focused on her, and Mandy's heart started to thump. "You mean...you?"

"I'm buying it," A.J. stated.

"That's cool, man," Marc reached out and shook his hand. "When did this happen?"

"I bought it last week. I'm going to rent it out. You know, branch out. Be a landlord."

"Wow." Mandy wasn't sure how to handle the mix of feelings swarming through her at the moment: pride, surprise, awe. "That's great news, A.J. Will you keep your day job?" She gestured to the house.

His pleased smile grew deeper. "Of course. I'm not an office kind of guy. I just thought it was about time I set up for the future."

"Congratulations," Boston said. "That's a smart move."

"Thanks, man," A.J. countered.

"Boston owns a fourplex," Mandy put in.

"You guys are monsters. I don't own anything," Marc lamented. He was finished with his water so he shoved the empty bottle at Mandy. Mandy glared at him.

"They're smart." Mandy shoved the bottle back. "Time to start taking care of yourself. The trash is over there." She jerked her head in the direction of a few scattered boxes, filled with garbage.

Marc grumbled and headed toward the boxes.

"I'm so happy for you, A.J." Mandy turned to him. "That's really great."

"Thanks to you."

"Me?"

"You inspired me, baby doll."

A.J.'s green eyes held hers for a long time. An old pleasure echoed through Mandy she couldn't deny or ignore. She took a deep breath and finished the last of her water, her gaze moving to A.J.'s new house.

By the afternoon, the entire house began to darken with the walls filled in. Now, the only light streamed in from the vacancy above where the trusses would go tomorrow, and through the framed windows.

The job was nearly over and a vacancy wedged inside of Mandy. She tried to focus on the pleasant fact that they'd created A.J.'s house. That her first job had been a success—she'd carried her share of the load. And she'd met Boston.

Mandy marveled that they worked like a well-oiled machine the last few days of the job, the trusses fitting in place just right. She enjoyed Larry's music, and let Marc's chiding slide by without comment. Boston and A.J. talked about the business of being a landlord like they'd known each other for years, not weeks. It was fun to hear A.J. plan how he was going to finish the inside of the house. Boston offered his suggestions and so did Mandy. By the time the last piece of plywood was nailed in place on the roof, the sadness of leaving the site, of the team dismantling and going their separate ways had dwindled to a dull ache and Mandy was ready to move on to the next project.

Parting was bittersweet. With Marc scheduling their dad's framing crews, odds were that she'd work with some of them again, but she wasn't sure when. She'd miss Larry's raunchy antics. What would the work day be without A.J.'s gentlemanly gestures? At least she'd see Boston.

As dusk fell over the site and they piled into the truck for the last drive to the home office, Mandy sat in the cab, looking at the house, and memories flashed. She wished she could drag out the job a little longer, but good framers got in and out on schedule so that the overall timetable for the project wasn't compromised for those standing in line next.

Boston climbed in next to her and smiled. His musky scent filled the cab and her head, causing her heart to take a spin. "Hey." He surprised her with a kiss. His lips were warm and a little salty.

"Hey." Joy caused a satisfied sigh to warble from her chest. She leaned her head against his shoulder and closed her eyes. The truck swayed as the others climbed in the back, the guys' laughter mixing with the memories of the past few weeks running through her head.

"Let's get something to eat. Want to?" Boston asked.

Mandy nodded. She kept her eyes closed, enjoying the pictures of the job flashing in her head. She felt Marc get in, close the door, and start the engine. Who'd have thought, she mused, thinking about the first day she laid eyes on Boston, that he would be sitting next to her, that he'd kiss her and they'd be together?

Moved to touch him, she angled her head up and he looked at her. He shot a quick glance at Marc, reminding her that they shared the intimate spot with her brother, before he gave her another kiss.

Content, Mandy closed her eyes for the rest of the drive.

Next Job

"When can I get back to work?" Mandy asked Marc. Six weeks had gone by since they'd wrapped her first framing job, and she was itching to get her hands on some wood. She missed the sweat, the scents and the hard work.

The weeks had been fun in the interim. Boston had been assigned to another crew and he'd asked her to meet him each day so they could take off for lunch together. She'd spent her days either at the bookstore or hanging with Cam when he wasn't working day shifts. She'd also enrolled for fall classes at the local college to start her GE classes that would eventually lead to her contractor's license.

"You can start tomorrow," Marc said. It was early evening; he'd just gotten home from a meeting with their dad. He was his usual cranky self as he poured himself a snack of Captain Crunch cereal.

"Dad must love the sales," she said, getting the milk out of the refrigerator and handing it to him.

"Yeah. Only four more houses to go and the development will close. But the pressure, man, I had to hire five new framers this week."

"So you'll be overseeing everything to make sure the quality is—"

"You don't have to tell me how to do my job,

Mand." He poured some milk.

"I know. You do a great job, you really do," she said, pulling out a barstool next to him. They both sat.

He was trying really hard not to smile and let the pleasure show on his face, Mandy could tell. She grinned, reached over and plucked an orange nugget of cereal from his bowl.

His eyes cut to hers in a teasing glare. "Get your own."

"You going out with Lar tonight?" she asked. He shrugged, spooned and chewed. "What? You two not making the rounds anymore?"

"He's making them. You know Larry." He paused. "I'm out of that scene, at least for a while anyway."

"I'm proud of you. You want to come to the bookstore with me and Boston tonight?"

He let out a good-natured sneer. "Don't push it."

"I thought you said you could appreciate a babe anywhere. There are babes at the bookstore, you know. You might do well with an intellectual type."

"Like I care if she's interested in my brain."

Mandy plucked another piece of cereal from his bowl. "You care or you'd be hanging with Lar tonight."

"What I care about is eating this bowl of cereal right now. Don't you have something to do, like read a book or something?" He lifted the nearly empty bowl and drank down the orangey milk.

"You can camouflage all you want Marcus, but I know you. You're tired of disposable. You're ready for a keeper."

"Who asked you?"

"Sister's intuition." Mandy tapped her temple. "Try

the bookstore. You never know," she said, standing, stretching. She looked at her watch: one more hour until she saw Boston again. "So, tomorrow, work. Yes! I've been dying to get back."

"Well, then, your dreams are about to come true."

Because Marc was now overseeing all of the houses under construction, Mandy didn't drive with him to the development. She liked having her own car, anyway. That way, she could meet up with Boston at lunch. He was a guy who approached things conservatively. Every decision from investments to what he ate was done with thought. Mandy loved to tease him about his healthy eating choices, while he equally enjoyed trying to convince her to convert to the other side.

The morning was warmer than usual, even for late August. The air felt as if temperatures were going to skyrocket. She opened the sunroof and let the hot beams bathe her. From her CD player, something jumpy blasted, and her nerves ticked thinking about the new job.

She'd worked with the best crew already, she doubted this group of guys could top the fun camaraderie she'd felt with A.J., Larry, Marc, and Boston. That was a given. But it really didn't matter. She was excited about the work, about building, watching yet another home rise from the dust.

With a smile on her lips, she pulled up to the site. The area buzzed like a beehive, and her stomach fluttered in anticipation. A large truck with a load of wood was parked in front of the cement foundation. Men she didn't recognize were unloading the lumber and carrying it to piles outside the groundwork. She couldn't wait to inhale the natural scent.

One *Haynes* truck was parked on the street as well as a handful of other trucks. Not knowing any of the new crew didn't bother her. She was there to learn, and the variety in foremen and their techniques was nearly as vast as the variety in home designs and floor plans.

She got out, went around to her trunk, and fetched her tool belt. She'd worn khaki shorts and a white tee shirt today figuring she'd spring her tanning attire on the crew once she knew them better.

After she secured her belt, she jogged onto the site. One of the workers, an older man with gray hair and black glasses, smiled at her. She waved. There was no need to feel butterflies. These guys all knew who she was, but the butterflies were there, stuck in her stomach anyway. She just hoped she wouldn't have to jump any hurdles like she had on her first job.

Two young guys in jeans and ratty tee shirts passed her as they hauled a load of two-by-fours closer to the cement floor. Both spared her a quick glance. One nodded his head in greeting at her.

Mandy nodded back with a smile.

Another guy, his bald head gleaming in the morning sun, frowned at her as he dropped a box of supplies on the ground near the foundation. Mandy just smiled at him.

The gray-haired man was shouting instructions to the lumber truck driver, now backing out the truck. When the last lumber was moved and the truck went on its way, he strode over.

"You must be Mandy." He stuck out his hand and they shook. "I'm Ben."

"Nice to meet you, Ben." Mandy eyed the growing lumber pile and took a deep breath.

"You like this, don't you?" Ben asked with a fatherly grin. "Never have worked with a woman framer before, this'll be a first. I was told you were a pro, and that we're lucky to have you on our team."

Mandy's eyes widened. "You were?"

"Yup."

But her dad would never brag like that, knowing how she prided herself on not using nepotism. And Marc giving her any kind of public compliment was out of the question. "Well, I can't imagine who told you that, but I'll try to live up to it," she said.

"And I was told not to give you any special allowances, that you could carry your weight and then some."

"Sure, yes. I can."

"All the same," Ben leaned close. The smell of his sweat tickled Mandy's nose. "If the guys give you any trouble, you come to me. Understand?"

What a difference between Ben and Marc, Mandy mused, smiling. "Sure. Thanks, Ben. But I'm sure I can handle the guys." The pressure was on, but she relished proving herself. She set her hands on her tool belt, ready to work.

"Where do you want me?" she asked.

"How about right over here?" The friendly, low tone rolled through her body and awakened her senses. She whirled around.

A.J. stood behind her. His green eyes twinkled over a

grin. "Hey, baby doll."

Mandy's heart started to thump. She smiled. "Hey. Good to see you, A.J."

A.J. had on shorts and a blue tee shirt. A red bandana was wrapped around his head. He reached out and tapped the tip of her nose with his finger. "You too. How's it going?"

"Great." Mandy's thumping heart started to slow. "How's the house? Homeownership agreeing with you?"

They started in the direction of the cement foundation. "It's agreeing with me just fine. So, you're working on this crew."

She nodded, then gestured with a tilt of her head to the other workers. "Think they'll give me a fight?"

"Nah." A.J. dug out his nail gun. "Come on, baby doll. Show 'em what you can do."

Jennifer Laurens writes novels for young adults from the office of her Pleasant Grove, Utah home. She has six children.

Other Titles:

Falling for Romeo
Magic Hands

ISBN: 978-1-933963-86-0
9 781933 963860 51099